Running
To Paradise

Running To Paradise

Frances Winfield Bremer

PROSPECT
PRESS

Sistersville, WV
New York, NY

With love and thanks
to Jer, who shared it all.

Published by Prospect Press
609 Main Street
Sistersville, West Virginia 26175

Library of Congress Catalog Number: 00-131297

ISBN: 1-892668-24-6

Manufactured in the United States of America

First Edition

10 9 8 7 6 5 4 3 2 1

A M D G

"The wind is old and still at play
While I must hurry on my way,
For I am running to Paradise."

W. B. Yeats

Chapter One :

Advent

T HIS WON'T BE EASY. I've always resisted the idea
of keeping a journal. I think it's important to
put that down at the very beginning, because if this
journal is to have any value it has to be completely
honest. No deletions. No phoniness.

At seminary someone suggested we keep a
prayer journal to record our spiritual progress. Prayers
offered and prayers answered. You could read back
over it and see how far you'd come.

I never liked the idea but maybe I was just afraid,
afraid that it might not show progress, afraid that I

might not have any great big obvious answers to prayer. Afraid that God wouldn't answer me as often or as quickly as he answered the others.

But now I need to keep a runner's journal because I'm training for a marathon. The training plan I have insists you note down each run, your time, the distance, the weather, how you were feeling etc., so I'm going to try to combine the two, running and prayer. That's the only way I know how to run anyway.

No time for a run until late afternoon and then I almost got caught by the darkness. Ran 4 miles along the river, 2 out, 2 back. Time? 32 minutes, 7 seconds. Weather? Cold! The air smelled like snow and the river had that greasy look it gets when there's a fine layer of ice forming on the surface. Prayed the Rosary, the Joyful Mysteries. Felt good, clean, excited about Advent, but I don't know how long this will last.

If I were the devil – actually I'm an agnostic on the subject of the devil – but if I were the devil, I'd twist Advent into a time of pressure and depression. Funny thing, that's just what it becomes for a lot of people, including priests. We're human too.

Lord. help me help the people of St. Anne's stay focused on the birth of your Son.

Father Frank clicked SAVE on his computer and put the document he had just created into a new file called **Journal.** Then he shut down, stood up and stretched. Thirty minutes later, after praying night prayer from the *LITURGY OF THE HOURS,* he turned off his bedside light and tried to put the day to rest.

But it had been a long complicated day, and parts of it kept replaying in his mind.

The door to St. Anne's was unlocked when Father Frank had arrived that morning to set up for 8 o'clock Mass. It swung open when he inserted his key but there were no lights on inside.

"George," Frank thought. "He's in here somewhere."

George was a parishioner of St. Anne's and a binge drinker, who always got a bad conscience afterwards and wanted to pray the Stations of the Cross, whether the church was open or not. Since the brass lock on the main door was old and corroded it was easy to force.

When Frank entered the church a shaft of pale morning light was shining through a stained glass window, illuminating three of the Stations on the right wall: number 9, "Jesus falls for the Third Time", number 10, "Jesus is Stripped of His Garments" and number 11, "Jesus is Nailed to the Cross."

George, middle-aged and unshaven, wearing a rumpled tweed coat and a baseball cap, was standing in front of number 11, a graphic close-up of the palm of Jesus' hand being nailed through to the horizontal bar of a cross still lying on the ground. The nailer was a nondescript man with a determined expression on his face. Just doing my job, you could almost hear him say.

Frank didn't know whether George identified with Jesus or the nailer of His hand at that moment, but that wasn't Frank's business. That was between God and George.

"Morning, Father." George snatched off his baseball cap and glanced nervously back towards the open door.

"Stay for Mass, George? You can light the candle on the Advent Wreath."

George stayed, the first time he'd stayed for Mass in the two years that Father Frank had been associate pastor at St. Anne's.

What George had thought of the homily he heard was anybody's guess, but Frank could see that his words made many people uncomfortable. He could read that on their faces.

The priesthood, Father Frank constantly reminded himself, was not a popularity contest.

Frank had chosen to preach on the first reading of the day which was from Isaiah 63: *Why do you let us wander, 0 Lord, from your ways, and harden our hearts so that we fear you not?*

As usual Father Frank delivered his homily striding back and forth at the front of the sanctuary. This Sunday he wore purple, which matched the purple alter cloth behind him. Purple was the ancient color for Advent and Lent.

Frank didn't use a microphone when he preached because he had found that his voice carried from the front of St. Anne's to the farthest pews in the back. This was thanks to his professional training as a sportscaster right after college, although if anyone had told him back then that someday he'd be using his "media voice" to deliver homilies he would have been amazed.

"Today is the first Sunday of Advent," he began. "Advent comes from 'adventus', the Latin word for 'coming.' The coming we're waiting for is Christ's at Christmas. So Advent is a time of waiting. That's hardest for kids, isn't it?"

Scattered nods in the pews.

"Actually, I think Advent is harder for adults. Why?"

He could see people shift restlessly, probably thinking of all they had to do before now and Christmas.

"Because there's something else going on during Advent." Sweat began to form on Frank's forehead as he spoke.

"We become a bit more attuned to God at this time of year," Frank said, "and that can be uncomfortable because it strips away at the hardness around our own hearts. There's pain and vulnerability underneath which we're used to anesthetizing with layers of concrete or steel or whatever grotesque metaphor you want to use for the hardness that seems to keep a heart from hurting."

His own heart was pounding by now because the words were so important. Easy does it, he told himself.

"The irony is," he continued, "the pain is not what kills you. That's good pain, the kind Christ came to heal, the kind He longs to ease with His tender open heart."

"It's the hardness of your hearts that will kill you. Hardness of heart is the hidden malignancy. You feel fine, but you're dying inside."

People didn't like the word "malignancy"; Frank could see that but he pushed his point home.

"Use me, please . . . to help God heal that malignancy with his love and forgiveness."

He was pleading now. "Maybe you don't need help, but maybe you know people outside the church who do. Bring them for counseling anytime during Advent. Don't let them walk around with a malignancy inside."

"That was a pretty tough message for Advent," his boss, Father O'Donnell, remarked over lunch in the rectory afterwards. "People don't need a cancer scare just before Christmas."

"Don't they?" Frank tried not to sound defensive

and concentrated on eating until he could think of something else to talk about.

As usual Ruthie, Father O'Donnell's border collie, broke the awkwardness. She had been edging her nose towards the tray with sandwiches on it at the far end of the old oak table when Father O'Donnell called out: "Here girl!"

He beckoned her with a piece of cheese from his own plate and his hand trembled as he stretched it out. Frank saw the tremble. He studied his boss out of the corner of his eye while Father O'Donnell fed the dog off his plate, ignoring Frank.

The pastor of St. Anne's was in his seventies, white-haired and sunken-eyed. He was ready to retire, had been for several years, but there was a priest shortage. So he stayed on at St. Anne's, letting Frank carry more and more of the workload.

Frank was eager to shoulder that load but he bristled when Father O'Donnell voiced any criticism, which he often did. "Why am I so thin skinned?" Frank wondered. Father O'Donnell had been a priest longer than Frank had been alive. He was a fine man and he'd earned the right to his opinions.

Mercifully, the telephone rang, and Frank went to answer it.

"The twins are here!" It was Mike, Frank's brother-in-law. "Three weeks early, but everybody's fine. They finally had to do a C section this morning."

"Advent babies!" Frank laughed. "Boys? Girls?"

"One of each. Will you do the baptisms? Claire wants to jump to the head of the line on your schedule."

"Think I'd let another priest near them? Give me Claire's number." Frank had spent the next hour talking to his older sister and his ecstatic mother and father who were grandparents for the first time. They all lived upstate where Frank grew up and the baptisms would be performed at Sacred Heart, Frank's old parish church. Of course he'd stay for the party afterwards and then spend the night at home.

The baby girl was Catherine Marie, named after both grandmothers, and the baby boy was Francis Joseph, named after Frank. He'd felt absurdly pleased when he heard this. It was almost as if he'd had a son of his own.

Frank felt the glow of it all afternoon as he worked to finalize the Advent schedule at St. Anne's. Francis Joseph, wonder what he'll look like, wonder if anyone will ever call him "Tom"?

Tom was Frank's nickname, one he disliked, and one that his priest friends rubbed in at every opportunity. It had started in seminary when someone said he looked like the actor Tom Cruise and it had stuck. Frank didn't see the resemblance himself but apparently other people did including the waitress who had seated him that night at Luigi's. When one of his friend's called out, "Hey Tom, you're late!" she did a double-take.

Celebrating the first Sunday in Advent with dinner at Luigi's was a tradition among the four priests. They had been at seminary together and were now all associate pastors in the diocese.

This was a night to relax before the countdown to Christmas, and Frank could see when he arrived that he was already a couple glasses of Chianti behind.

"Sorry, I was running."

"From your fans?" This remark came from Bill who was sitting across the table. He was a big tough-looking former Marine who had not only converted to Catholicism in his forties but gone on to become a priest. Takes me a while longer than most people, Father Bill always said, but I get there eventually.

The other two were younger, in their mid-thirties like Frank. Charlie on his left was thin with red hair and a bushy red beard. Brian seated to Frank's right had curly brown hair and deep blue eyes behind his glasses.

They were at a corner table in their favorite Italian restaurant on Route 1. Luigi's was convenient, cheap and rich with the smells of garlic and olive oil.

Frank poured himself a glass of wine and quickly changed the subject. "Anybody catch the Patriot's game?"

"Torture, pure torture! Bledsoe couldn't throw worth a damn."

"It wasn't his fault," Bill leaned forward and rocked the table with his beefy arms. "The pass protection stank! The quarterback can't play the game alone can he?"

"Why doesn't Pete Carroll trade some of those guys for a decent front line?"

"Why don't they sack Carroll and get Parcells back?"

They had talked football for a while, then switched to food. Charlie said that he made better *fettucine carbonara* than Luigi but the others disagreed and so everyone ordered a second helping for comparison purposes.

They drank two more bottles of red wine, got sentimental over the death of Mother Teresa whom Brian had met as a seminarian in Calcutta, and someone suggested that the cardinal should give younger priests more responsibilities.

"And add a few more hours to the day," Frank had said. "A cardinal can do that, can't he?"

"Sure Tom, when you're a cardinal you can take that up with God."

Over coffee, expresso chocolate cheesecake and cigars, they decided to settle for once and for all whether Vatican II had been a triumph or a disaster for the Catholic Church.

Finally at midnight, Luigi himself came to their table and said it was closing time and that he'd called taxis to take them home. They hadn't noticed that the tables around theirs had gradually emptied. First the families with young children had bundled up the kids and left, then the older couples had pulled on their parkas and wool hats and gone from the warmth of Italy into the cold New England night.

"Come again." Luigi waved them out the door.

"Just keep coming," he called after them. "Gives me good feelings to see you enjoy yourselves. Bless you, Fathers."

Back in his room at St. Anne's, Frank realized he was tired. He had just enough energy to make the first entry in his running journal before ending the day as he almost always did, as every Catholic priest all over the world vows to do every night: praying night prayer from the *LITURGY OF THE HOURS*:

"All-powerful God, increase our strength of will for doing good that Christ may find an eager welcome at His coming and call us to His side in the kingdom of heaven, where He lives and reigns with You and the Holy Spirit, one God, for ever and ever. Amen."

Chapter Two:

Midnight Mass

DECEMBER 23RD STARTED EARLY for Father Frank. Before the sun was up he headed out the front door of the rectory for a four-mile run.

St. Anne's faced Niantic Avenue and a row of old clapboard houses most of which had been divided into apartments. George lived in one of them with his wife and step-child, but there were no lights on in their apartment at this hour. All was peaceful.

The only other person awake in the parish was Danny in the gas station across Route 1. Frank crossed at the light and waved to Danny as he ran by. Then he turned right onto the road that bordered the river. It had a good smooth surface and little traffic at this time of day.

Frank increased his speed to an 8 minute pace and began to pray one of the Jesus prayers. This morning it was *Jesus – Christ have – mercy – on us* repeated rhythmically with each breath he took.

Prayer was necessary to Father Frank as the oxygen he breathed. It fed his soul and united him to God. Now, as he ran, he prayed for the parishioners of St. Anne's, then for his own family, and for Father O'Donnell who was down with the flu. He finished the way he always did on his morning run: *Lord, give me strength enough, sense enough, and most of all, love enough to do Your will today.*

After two miles Frank turned around and headed back and, although his legs kept going, his thoughts became more pedestrian. He badly needed a new pair of running shores if he were going to get serious about a marathon.

Every year his parents gave him a check for Christmas and Frank had just about decided to spend the money on a good pair of Nikes. He might check them out at the mall this afternoon, *if* he got to the mall this afternoon with everything else that was going on.

Streaks of golden light began to appear in the sky and the icy river picked them up and threw them back to the bare trees that stood silhouetted along the edge of the road.

Danny was unplugging the flashing Christmas lights that circled the gas station when Frank passed him on the way home. Dark figures, wrapped up against the cold, were emerging from the houses across Niantic Avenue. Morning had risen by the time Frank finished his run.

He celebrated both the 8:00 and noon Masses and then, after lunch, went over to the school to watch the dress rehearsal for the St. Anne's Nativity play.

The rehearsal turned out to be a disaster. The combination of excited children, a real baby and live animals was always potentially volatile, but ironically it was the oldest member of the cast who set off the explosion.

She was an 8th grade angel whose job was to bring glad tidings of great joy to all people, and this she did beautifully with hands pressed together and eyes looking straight out at the empty chairs in the school's all-purpose room. But then her attention strayed to one of the shepherds, her youngest brother, who was trying to keep the family dog from wiggling out of his sheep costume.

"Don't choke him, Kevin!" she hissed. "Let go! You're choking him!"

Kevin let go, but when the dog became a dog again he immediately began poking his nose into the manger where interesting smells were coming from the vicinity of Baby Jesus.

This year's Baby Jesus had been supplied by Liz, who alternated with Susie in providing a new baby for the Nativity play every year. Some of the other mothers at St. Anne's felt it was unfair that these two always got to have their babies play Jesus, but for the last several years Liz and Susie's sons and daughters had behaved impeccably, either sleeping through the whole thing, or waving their arms and legs in the air. Usually Baby Jesus was not the problem. This year he was, in an indirect way.

As soon as he felt the dog's cold nose under his blanket the baby kicked his chubby legs with all his strength (he was really too big for the part), tipped himself out of the cardboard box that served as a manger and onto the Virgin Mary's lap. Then he rolled onto the floor where straw poked him in the face, and he started to scream.

Now the Virgin Mary, who was only six, began to cry too because, even though she knew that this actually wasn't the real Jesus, she'd never been in a play before and she got confused about what was real and what wasn't. And here was Jesus lying face down in front of her, wailing.

Finally Liz had to come on stage and pick up her baby. She realized at once that he needed to be changed so she whisked him off-stage right, followed by the dog.

Then, on cue, the Three Kings arrived from the Orient. Since they had been traveling from afar they didn't know what had happened. So when they got on stage to present their gifts to an empty manger it struck the three nine year old boys as so funny that they delivered their gold, frankincense and myrrh snickering and nudging each other. "Stop it!" the bossy angel whispered loudly, twice, but to no effect, so she climbed off her perch on the roof of the stable and smacked the biggest King, another brother, in the head.

"Curtain!" called Father Frank who was leaning against a wall, laughing. He signaled to two teenagers and after a moment's pause a dark blue sheet rippled across the room, cutting off the Nativity scene from the row of folding chairs where the audience would sit that night.

"We're going to have to start it all over again," Liz apologized as she poked her head through the opening with Baby Jesus still in her arms, but by this time Frank was laughing so hard that all he could do was nod.

"Frank?" A young man came up to him. He was dressed in outdoor clothes and carried a duffel bag.

"Oh Steve, I'm sorry," Frank pulled himself together. "We were expecting you this afternoon. Thanks for coming." Frank clapped the tall fair-haired seminarian on the shoulder. "Boy do I need your help!"

Steve had done an internship at St. Anne's the

previous summer and was back to assist Father Frank over Christmas.

"Want to look into the church before we go to the rectory?"

"Thanks."

Steve followed Frank out of the school and across to the church.

"All the decorating's done tomorrow for Midnight Mass, so it looks sort of bare now, doesn't it?" Frank said.

Indeed, St. Anne's was colorless except for the red candle glowing to signal that there were consecrated elements in the tabernacle. Someone had placed a plastic baby bottle with a sprig of holly in front of the statue of Mary which was in a niche on the front left of the church. But the statue of Joseph, who was leaning his stone arms on a rough piece of carpentry in a niche on the right, was completely unadorned.

"Wait til tomorrow," Frank said. "Wait until Midnight Mass."

The next day, Christmas Eve, there was no real routine. The Mass schedule had been cleared to give everyone time to decorate the church and parishioners were coming in and out all day through a constant snowfall. They also brought small presents for the priests:

poinsettias, fruitcakes, and religious pictures some of which Frank considered hideous but didn't say so. And as usual there was mistletoe from Brenda who had a crush on Frank.

"Don't encourage her," Father O'Donnell snapped from his sick bed.

"She doesn't need encouragement," Frank replied and Steve, who was standing in the doorway, muttered, "I'm taking notes on how you handle this, Frank."

"Don't send anyone Christmas cards, and absolutely no presents," the old priest said and slumped down in his bed. The collar of his rumpled blue pajamas bunched up around his ears.

"Cards and presents to parishioners only cause problems. Someone always gets upset. Learned that years ago."

"Right," said Frank. "I'm going up to the mall to finish shopping for my family. Need anything?"

Father O'Donnell frowned and shook his head.

When he arrived at the mall Frank had to circle the underground garage three times before he found a place to park. He looked at his watch as he got into the elevator. Why did he always leave shopping until Christmas eve? Next year he wouldn't.

The crowd in the elevator pushed him out onto the main floor, right in front of a group of children who were being entertained by a chorus of animated bears while they waited to sit on Santa's lap. Santa himself looked tired and irritable, and some of the children hung back when their turn came.

Bears? When did bears become a Christmas symbol? Maybe he should buy toy bears for the twins.

Frank went into one of the bigger stores and found the baby department, but after looking at bears of all sizes, he decided on pink and blue teething rings as more practical. Then he bought photo albums for Claire and Mike and his parents.

He checked his watch again. There wasn't much time.

He walked back out into the mall towards the sports store on the other side, glanced at the Nikes in the window, and then, in flagrant violation of Father O'Donnell's rule against presents for parishioners, Frank ducked into Victoria's Secret and made a purchase. "Don't bother to wrap it, I'm in a hurry," he said impatiently, waiting for his change. He was glad now that he'd put on jeans and a sweater and had left his clerics at home.

Back in the elevator he was struck by the tense expression on people's faces. "I must look that way too," he thought. "It's contagious."

It took him a long time to find his car in the underground garage.

Between St. Anne's and the river there was a row of small two room cottages which had housed mill workers back when the mill was operating. Some of them were still inhabited. After he left the mall Frank crossed town and drove down the river road and pulled up in front of the last cottage on the left.

The house was dark when he rang the doorbell but after a minute the front light came on, a face appeared at the window, and then, after a few more minutes the front door opened.

An old woman stood in the doorway dressed in a flannel nightgown and a sweater.

"Father Frank! Where's your Roman collar?"

"In my room. I'm disguised like everyone else." Frank stepped inside and closed the door behind himself. No sense letting the cold in.

"Merry Christmas, Mrs. Abernathy." He felt suddenly shy as he handed her the Victoria's Secret bag. "I'm running so late I didn't have time to wrap it."

Mrs. Abernathy's arthritic hands reached for the bag, but before she looked inside she felt inside and her puzzled expression softened as she touched the contents.

She pulled out a white bathrobe which was so irresistibly fleecy that she put it on right then and there over her sweater. Only when she had tied the belt firmly around her waist did she look up at Frank again, and when she did there were tears in her eyes.

"You shouldn't have spent your money on me." The tears rolled down her cheeks and she brushed them away and laughed at herself.

"Forgive me," he said, still shy. "The last time I was here I was afraid you'd freeze to death."

"Go on, Father Frank! I'm too tough to freeze," she said, stroking the fleece with one hand and smoothing back her thin white hair with the other.

"I have to go. . . Midnight Mass," he explained and opened the door. She watched him from the window as he hurried to his car and drove back to St. Anne's.

At 11:30 on Christmas Eve St. Anne's was two-thirds full and by ten minutes to midnight there was standing-room only. Father Frank could see into the church from a small window in the door of the sacristy behind the altar where he and Steve were vesting for Mass, assisted by Liz's oldest son who, as altar boy, was learning about the vestments.

"This is an alb," Frank said, pulling on a long white robe with sleeves over his black cassock. Then he tied a rope called a cincture around his waist. Next Frank took a narrow strip of embroidered cloth, a stole, which he kissed before he draped it around his neck.

"Why kiss it?"

"Reverence. It's a symbol of priestly ministry. Hand me the chasuble, Steve."

Steve handed him an ivory colored sleeveless cloak with tapestry panels in red, green, and gold. Frank pulled it over the stole, adjusted it around his shoulders and smoothed down the panels, then sighed with relief.

Finally, at last, after all the preliminaries, he was ready for Midnight Mass. Frank and Steve joined the procession from the back of the church.

O come all ye faithful, joyful and triumphant. The organ surged and the choir and congregation lifted their voices, *O come ye, O come ye, to Beth- eth- lehem. Come and Behold Him, born the King of Angels. O come, let us adore Him, O come let us adore Him, O come let us adore Him, Christ, the Lord!*

Father Frank opened the Mass in the name of the Father, and the Son, and the Holy Ghost, led the congregation in the confession of sins, and then joined them in singing the Gloria:

Glory to God in the highest, and peace to his people on earth. Lord God, heavenly King, almighty God and Father, we worship you, we give you thanks, we praise you for your glory,

Lord Jesus Christ, only Son of the Father, Lord God, Lamb of God, you take away the sin of the world: have mercy on us; you are seated at the right hand of the Father: receive our prayer.

For you alone are the Holy One, you alone are the Lord, you alone are the Most High, Jesus Christ, with the Holy Spirit, in the glory of God the Father. Amen.

As he sang the Gloria, Father Frank looked back at the people in the pews. He could see that some St. Anne's families had doubled or tripled in size with visiting relatives and he also saw with gladness that there were many strangers who had come as couples or by themselves.

Children, up long past their bedtime, wiggled in their parents' arms or stared with sleepy fascination at the brilliant red poinsettias that filled every niche of the church and circled the giant wooden crucifix behind the altar. The lights hanging from the ceiling glowed warm and golden, in contrast with the stained glass windows, usually so colorful, which were now blackened by the night sky behind them.

Soon it was time for the Alleluia, and then the Gospel reading of the familiar passage from St. Luke about Mary giving birth to Jesus in a stable because there was no room for them in the inn.

Then came Father Frank's homily, which he intentionally kept upbeat and positive because he knew it was his one chance to reach people who might never come back, including a friend from the Y where he worked out on days he didn't run. Father Frank was surprised and pleased to see Christopher sitting in the back of the church.

He tried not to focus his homily on anything negative but on God's eternal Christmas offering in a tiny, vulnerable, human baby who incarnates a Love which everyone has the freedom to reject, or to receive. Father Frank held out the hope that some might, that night, accept this Love for the very first time.

The service now moved to the Eucharist, the most sacred part of the Mass. Bread and wine had been brought up by Liz and her husband and children. Steve circled the altar three times with a thurible full of incense which wafted out when he swung the chain, the sweet smell slowly permeating St. Anne's as Father Frank performed the consecration:

Lord, accept our gifts on this joyful feast of our salvation. By our communion with God made man, may we become more like Him who joins our lives with Yours, for he is Lord for ever and ever. Amen.

And suddenly, without seeking it, Frank had a very real sense of the presence of angels and saints and of Christ himself, a little taste of what was going to make the sacrifices of his priesthood worthwhile: eternity with God.

It took a long time to serve communion to so many people. Frank and Steve stood in front of the center aisle and eight Eucharistic Ministers fanned out across the church but the lines seemed endless and Frank could tell, by their tentativeness, that in them were also some non-Catholics who wanted to receive the sacred body and blood of Christ, so he gave it to them.

This festive Mass celebrating the birth of the Savior was not a time to be legalistic, Frank thought. It was a time to be *inclusive*, to reach out to all members of the human family who came forward. Tonight Father Frank's faith would stand in the gap of any unbelief.

Finally, after the Allelulia chorus from Handel's *Messiah* had been sung, it was over. Slowly, slowly the church emptied and the last "Merry Christmas" was called out by the last departing parishioner.

Frank and Steve returned their vestments to the sacristy, switched off the lights and walked through the snow to the rectory next door. A faint smell of incense followed in the air around them.

"Beer?" asked Steve as they stomped their boots outside the kitchen door.

"No," Frank answered. "I'm even too tired for beer tonight and we've got three more Masses in the morning. You go ahead though. Merry Christmas, Steve."

Frank walked wearily upstairs, checked on Father O'Donnell and then went into his own room. He had no strength left for a journal entry, or night prayer from the LITURGY OF THE HOURS.

He collapsed into an exhausted sleep and his last conscious image was of Mrs. Abernathy.

"Those were your tears, Jesus," he said softly.

Chapter Three:

Epiphany

R AN 4 1/2 MILES through the old neighborhood, past Mary Jo's house. I wonder who lives there now? The weather? Cold, of course. At least the sidewalks were pretty well cleared. My feelings? That's part of a longer story . . .

Today was my day off so I drove home to watch the playoffs with Dad. The Patriots lost and the worse they did the more morose he became. How many million football games have I watched on that couch in our basement?

How many times did Mary Jo and I make

love on that couch in our basement, very very quietly after my parents were all the way upstairs in bed? "Quiet as a mouse," I'd whisper in her ear, and she'd laugh.

We became sexually active senior year in high school and really wrestled with it because we were both Catholics. It was important to be able to say we loved each other before we took that step. I wrestled with that the same way I wrestle with everything. If not abide by all the rules, at least be straight about the guilt.

And there was lots of guilt, but I didn't just stumble into the relationship. In my mind, as a senior in high school, love was a decision. I was making a commitment to her. Someday we would probably get married. But it didn't work out that way, did it Lord?

At college I began dating other women, sleeping with other women, so there went the commitment part, but I can't remember exactly when the guilt stopped. Maybe it never really stopped but just got buried under the sex, the drinking, and all the mental and spiritual pollution that I was wallowing in and loving. We had the stereo and the TV on all the time (when did we ever study?) and we rented a lot of videos, the more graphic the better. We were cool, Jesus. You weren't. And I soon got bored with Mary Jo, too. I didn't want her hanging around me anymore, reminding me of the altar boy I had been.

I stopped going to Mass, mostly because I was just too lazy, but looking back I can see that there was something else happening too. I was trying to avoid You. Just the thought of You made me uncomfortable so I pushed You away, stuck You in the back of a bureau drawer with the green Scapular Dad had given me.

I haven't thought about that Scapular for a long time. It's probably still around somewhere. I remember Dad telling Claire and me that all Catholics have an obligation to at least consider the religious life, and I guess the Scapular – a green silk cord with a picture of Mary holding the Infant Jesus that I wore around my neck under my shirt, for a while anyway – was his way of trying to bind us to that possibility as we left for college. I'm not sure Mom agreed, but she went along with it at the time. And maybe it worked.

But I've never been further away from thoughts of the religious life than when I moved to New York after graduation. I'd majored in communications and loved sports, so big time sportscaster here I come.

The work wasn't too exciting though, most

of the time you're sitting around in airless studios interviewing overpaid athletes, and hanging onto their every word as if they were imparting pearls of wisdom, which they weren't.

TV shows look so glamorous when you watch them at home, but when you're right there in the studio you find out how phony they are. A studio's a dark cavernous place in some big building, with a couple of armchairs and a table on a platform, and maybe some sports posters or a plastic geranium hanging on a prop wall behind to give it warmth. But in back of that little inner wall, and all around the tasteful looking interviewing area, there's nothing. Nothing. Just empty space where technicians scurry around pulling wires and aiming cameras, but they know all sorts of tricks to make it look real and solid and important.

Actually, I fit right in there, because behind my physical appearance there was nothing important going on either, nothing real or solid anymore. But I was good looking and looks were everything, weren't they? "God, I envy you your looks," my boss said.

So, the only thing I really cared about in those days was myself; getting ahead and having fun. There were plenty of women who were eager to go to bed with me, and there was always plenty of booze.

I never even went inside a church anymore, but every Sunday, without fail, I'd call Mom and Dad and tell them how great things were going for me. I wonder if they believed me?

I wonder if they were praying for me? They probably were because my life was about to change dramatically, first for the worse, then slowly, slowly for the better. That's the way You work, isn't it, Lord? Break us down so You can make us whole.

One day Mary Jo came to New York with a diamond ring on her finger. She was engaged to some guy in Boston. I felt betrayed. What about her commitment to me?

"What commitment?" she asked. "I don't even know the person you are anymore."

She was right. Anyway, marriage didn't fit into my immediate plans. It would take me out of circulation, and probably screw up my career because Mary Jo was old-fashioned and would freak out if she knew what went on in the media world.

I guess I forgot about her again for a while, because when Mom sent me a clipping from our home town paper showing Mary Jo and her new husband in front of Sacred Heart I felt like I'd been hit in the solar plexus with a baseball bat.

I went down to the bar for a drink and three days later my boss tracked me down, hauled me out of there, dumped me in my apartment, and told me, on his way out the door, that I was fired.

So it's time to change my life. I looked at myself when I'd sobered up, and finally admitted that I wasn't a person I particularly liked. I was drinking more and more, not yet an alcoholic but on the way to being. I was 26 years old, and was settling into an empty, immoral lifestyle. I needed to go back to my roots to find myself again.

Mom and Dad agreed to let me live at home until I decided what I wanted to do and the first thing I did when I got home was start going to Mass again. And I spent a lot of time reading in the black canvas chair up in my room.

I got a job and dated a couple of new women and then settled on one who was Catholic. She would have been the kind of person I would have married. My parents liked her. After dating her for about four months I had the feeling that yeah, I could do this, have a regular job, get married, all of that. After the kind of wild stuff that went before this was normal.

Then I started reading THE SEVEN STOREY MOUNTAIN by Thomas Merton, a book that had been gathering dust on my bookshelf for years, and You came crashing in on me.

I remember that it was about six o'clock in the evening and I could smell the dinner Mom was cooking in the kitchen and hear the murmur of the portable TV she had on the kitchen counter turned to the news. And in my book Merton's friend Lax was describing America as a country full of people wanting to be kind and pleasant and happy and serve You but not knowing how. These people were hoping to turn on the tube some day – in Merton's time it would have been a radio – and find someone who could tell them about Your love in a language that didn't sound hackneyed or crazy, but with the authority and conviction: the conviction born of sanctity.

SANCTITY. That was the word that jumped out at me. That's like being a saint, isn't it? Where does sanctity come from? There was no sanctity coming out of that TV downstairs.

"From YOU," You told me, so loud and clear that I threw down the book and fled from the room.

"What's going on?" Mom looked at me closely. As far as she knew I was working on my application to business school, while what I was really doing was messing around with Merton and sanctity and getting in so far over my head that I was hearing voices.

You know the rest of the story Lord. When it finally hit me a couple of weeks later, I remember it hit me in the shower. Kind of a baptismal scene I guess. I was trying to imagine my future, trying to imagine myself in five years, or ten years and the screen just went blank. The only thing I could picture myself doing was being a priest.

Well, that was my epiphany. You called me, and I answered yes. But You must have known what You were doing because when I ran past Mary Jo's old house today all I felt was happiness, and I prayed for her happiness too.

Chapter Four:

Ash Wednesday

B̲Y THE END OF FEBRUARY THE WEATHER was so cold and snowy that Father Frank did most of his running on a treadmill at the YMCA. There was a strict rule that anyone who used the Y's fitness center could spend only twenty minutes on each cardiovascular machine to give others a chance, so Frank worked out on the treadmill first, and then moved to the stationary bike.

The Y was packed wall to wall with sweating bodies at 7 o'clock in the morning and a young man climbed onto a bike only a couple of feet away from Frank's. It was Christopher, whom Frank had spotted in coat and tie in the back of St. Anne's at Midnight Mass while Frank was up at the altar in his vestments.

Now they were both dressed in shorts and t-shirts. They looked very much alike, except Chris was blond and wore Reeboks, while Frank was breaking in a new pair of Nikes.

Chris saw Frank's lips moving.

"Talking to yourself, Father Frank?"

"Hey Chris, what's up?" Frank asked.

"Trying to keep the old bod in shape," Chris laughed.

They synchronized the rhythm of their peddling so they could talk, although it wasn't easy to hear each other with the noise of the machines and the blaring TV overhead.

"I saw you at Midnight Mass," Frank said.

"Yeah, I just sort of ended up there. I told you that I wasn't raised with any religion. . ."

"Right."

"But once I met you, I guess I got curious."

"Have you tried other churches?"

"No, it's not that. I really haven't spent any time in churches at all. They never had any attraction."

"A lot of people feel that way. It's natural if you're not used to it."

"But I liked your Midnight Mass," Chris said.

"Great to see you there . . ." Frank panted. He was almost at the end of his workout.

"How do you do it?"

"Do what?"

"All of it?' Chris asked. "How do you do all of it? Run, work out, be a priest?"

"I've got a good coach."

Chris looked interested. "Yeah? I've been looking for a personal trainer." He leaned over closer.

"Does your guy have any free time?"

"Sure, all the time in the world." Frank grinned. "It's God."

He slowed to a cool-down pace, but Chris speeded up. Maybe he doesn't want to hear this, Frank thought. But Chris was still bending his head towards Frank, straining to make out his words.

"I remember in seminary my spiritual director asking me, what's your image of God? And I told him that I kind of think of God as a coach, giving you another twenty laps, upping the ante like a coach, always asking you to give more, and more and more. God is the one who supports you, brings out the best that's inside, but like any coach he's always raising the bar."

Frank got off his bike. He remembered that the expression on the face of his spiritual director, who had not been a sports-minded man, was a little like Chris' expression right now: startled and maybe slightly embarrassed by Frank's image of God as coach.

"Back to St. Anne's," Frank said. "Have a good workout, Chris."

Father Frank threaded his way across the crowded fitness center, showered and dressed in the men's locker-room, and just before 8:00 was vesting in the sacristy for the first Ash Wednesday Mass.

Ash Wednesday was an odd day, Frank always thought. A lot of people just wanted the ashes. They'd call the rectory first thing in the morning and say when can I get my ashes? I don't want to go to Mass, I just want my ashes. It was kind of perverse.

The ashes were a wonderful custom, a reminder of mortality, and the cycle of life, yet in the whole scheme of salvation they meant nothing compared to the Eucharist. But here were people coming out in droves for ashes and not wanting to go to Mass to get them. Sometimes Frank wanted to shake people . . . or cry for them.

"Lord, protect us in our struggle against evil," Father Frank began the Mass.

"As we begin the discipline of Lent, make this season holy by our self-denial. Grant this through our Lord Jesus Christ, you Son, who lives and reigns with you and the Holy Spirit, one God, for ever and ever."

"Amen," the congregation responded.

St. Anne's emptied quickly after Mass. Frank had just turned out the main lights and was walking down the center aisle, headed for the rectory and breakfast, when he heard sobs coming from a pew at the back of the church near the statue of the Sacred Heart.

He could dimly make out a woman's form. She was kneeling on a kneeler with her elbows propped on the pew in front and her face was buried in her hands. She was almost hidden in a scarf and winter coat but the light that surrounded the statue behind her lit up her long red hair hanging below her scarf.

"Patty?" He called down the pew. She nodded but didn't look up so he went in and sat down.

"Is it George?" he asked.

She nodded once more but kept her hands over her face.

"Can you tell me about it?"

"Oh, Father . . ." She began to cry again.

Frank sat there beside her, waiting, praying. He wasn't in a hurry. He could wait until she was ready to tell him what was wrong.

When Patty finally lifted her head and looked at him, Father Frank saw that the ashes he had pressed on her forehead just a few minutes ago with the words: "Remember you are dust and to dust you will return," were now mingled, in long black streaks, with the tears on her face.

"George didn't come home again last night," she said. "I thought he'd come today for ashes." Her voice took on an edge. "Where the hell is he Father?"

Frank knew the family who lived on the other side of Niantic Avenue. He had married Patty and George, the first wedding Frank had performed at St. Anne's.

He'd hope then that George, who was attending AA faithfully, would give Patty and her young daughter the security they needed. And, he'd hoped, that the marriage would be good for George, too. Settle him down.

"He's on the wagon, then he's off the wagon. I don't know how much more of this I can take." Patty poured out her frustrations.

Frank nodded as he listened.

"I understand," he said. "It must be so hard for you."

"God, when I think about the future it scares me, because I don't know if I can trust him. I never know which George I'm dealing with."

"That must be the worst of all."

"It is. It is!" She was silent again, with her forehead once more pressed on the back of the pew in front, and, as he sat there beside her, Frank became physically aware of the light from the statue behind them. He sensed it as a kind of balm easing Patty's pain, making it more bearable.

"I was sure he'd be at St. Anne's this morning. George loves this place," she said and looked back at Frank.

"He loves you and Kim, too. Hang in there Patty. God isn't finished with George, or any of us, yet."

She sighed and checked her watch. "Oh God, my shift starts in ten minutes!" She jumped up, pulled her scarf tight, and stuffed her long hair down the back of her coat.

"I've got to run, Father."

"Wait." Frank put out a hand to stop her. "Wait just a second."

He reached into his pocket and pulled out a white handkerchief. Then, still holding her arm with one hand, gently cleaned the ashy tears off her face with the other. With a quick "thank you," she was gone.

When he was alone in the church Frank walked around to the statue of the Sacred Heart that was glowing in its niche behind them.

The Risen Christ with his Sacred Heart exposed was an image that brought comfort to many Catholics, including Frank. But it made most non-Catholics avert their eyes, because Jesus was depicted wearing His heart on the outside: totally giving, totally loving, and open to all the pain in the world. That was hard for some people to look at.

That afternoon Father Frank had a meeting with the head of youth ministry. It did not go well. Choose your battles, they had said in seminary. Frank had had a running battle with Joyce, the head of youth ministry, since he'd been at St. Anne's. And he hadn't chosen it. At least not at the beginning.

Joyce had resented him since the day he arrived. She was an older single women and youth ministry had been her territory, and Frank's predecessor, Father Kevin, had been her ally. Still was. Frank knew that she often stopped by to see Kevin at his new parish, mostly to complain about Frank. There was a lot of back-biting which Frank hated.

Today they were supposed to plan the retreat for the teenagers which would be held in June. Joyce had chosen "Let Us Build the City of God" for the theme, which was a song the kids liked, but Frank didn't. He tried to very gently explain his thinking.

"Let's just be careful how we present it, Joyce. I know it's just a song but it's also basically a heresy that we can somehow earn our own salvation ourselves, rather than through God's grace. Is this what we want the teenagers to believe?"

Joyce looked at him like he was the kind of perfume she didn't like the smell of and pushed her chair farther away from his desk.

"You're going to completely ruin it."

"Ruin what?"

"The retreat. Why do you have to be so rigid?"

"I thought our role was to point them towards the truth?"

"You sound like a first year seminarian, Father." Her dark eyes mocked him. "And a spoil sport. Isn't the important thing that these kids are coming to something sponsored by St. Anne's instead of hanging out at the mall or doing drugs down by the river?"

"Then we're just glorified babysitters."

"Maybe we are, but they're all excited about it. They won't be for long if you start harping on heresy. They don't even know what the word means and if they did they couldn't care less. Life is tough for kids today."

"I know that," Frank looked down and noticed that his hands were balled into tight fists. He made a conscious effort to open them and tried to smile across his desk at Joyce.

"Tell me what they're so excited about."

"Well," she crossed her short legs, and leaned forward. "They want the whole retreat to have a kind of talk-show format, so everyone can open up and share their pain and maybe even cry if they want to without anyone making fun of them. Father Kevin and I have always dreamed of this. It will be very therapeutic, don't you think?"

"For the kids?"

"Who else?"

"I don't know, I'm just trying to figure this thing out. When are you going to have the Mass?"

"Oh no. No Mass. It takes too long. We want everybody to have time to really share with the others. Nobody has enough time to talk about their pain these days, you can tell that by just turning on your TV."

"Where's Christ in all of it?"

Joyce reacted as if she had been slapped in the face.

"You are going to ruin it, aren't you?"

"I just want to know what you're going to do with all their pain if you leave Christ out."

"We can be Christ to each other. We'll end with lots of hugs."

"The church isn't in the hug business. You might as well pass out Teddy Bears."

"People can come to Mass any old time. This will be something special. And," she fixed her black eyes on him. "You can share your pain with the group too, Father Frank. Then maybe they won't think of you as such a plastic priest."

That stung. Should he yield? Or should he stand for what he believed in? Pick your battles, they had said. They didn't say it would be easy.

"How about combining the two," he suggested. "The church combines the therapeutic and the sacramental all the time. It's a dynamite combination."

"Maybe," she shrugged as she got ready to leave. "I'll mention it to the kids, but I don't think they'll go for it. Times have changed, Father, even if some people haven't changed with them."

After he heard the front door of the rectory close behind her, Frank grabbed his parka from the back of his office door and whistled for Father O'Donnell's dog who came running from the kitchen with an eager look on her face.

"Walk? Come on Ruthie." Frank took her leash from a drawer in the hall table. "Let's get out of here."

His thoughts hurt as he walked down towards the river. Plastic priest? Do they really think that? Don't they know how much I care about them, how much their pain hurts me too?

Toughen up, he raged at himself. If you don't get a thicker skin you'll end up just one big ball of pain, and you won't be of any use to God, or anyone else.

Frank and Ruthie were now in sight of the old railway bridge that crossed the river below Mrs. Abernathy's house. He knew that some of the St. Anne's teenagers hung out under the rusted pilings that formed a kind of tunnel where the bridge met the riverbank.

He couldn't see whether there was anybody under the bridge now, but there were moving spots of bright color up along the dark side of the bridge itself. Kids in parkas, he realized as he continued further down road. St. Anne's kids? He couldn't tell from this distance but he was horrified that anybody thought a railroad bridge high over an icy river was a good place to hang out.

The cell phone in his pocket rang. He shifted Ruthie to his left side, fished out the phone and answered it on the third ring.

"Steve! Hi . . . No . . . walking the dog . . . How's it going? . . . Sure . . . I've got a meeting that usually ends around nine. I could meet with you after that. Can it wait 'til then? . . . . . Anything wrong? . . . okay . . . see you tonight."

"Let's go home," he said to Ruthie. "Father O'Donnell's going to be missing you."

Actually, Frank's meeting lasted until almost ten that evening. When he finally got back to his office he found Steve sprawled in his one arm chair, staring out the window where there was nothing to see but blackness.

"You okay?" Frank put his hand on Steve's shoulder.

"Not really. I don't know about this priesthood business." Steve looked up. "I don't think I'm going to make it, Frank."

Frank dropped into his desk chair. He saw that there were tears in Steve's blue eyes.

"What's going on?"

"I'm not sure I can talk about it," Steve said. "It's so hard," he paused then blurted out, "Frank, don't you ever want a woman?"

"Yes . . . sometimes."

"Then the desire doesn't go away?"

"No."

"Shit. I can't handle that! But it's not just that, it's everything else. The companionship with a woman, just being with her and sharing my life with her, and waking up with her every morning and going to bed with her every night, and growing old together, and having kids. Oh my God, I always wanted to have a lot of kids and go to their baseball games."

"I know," Frank said. "Me too."

"Then why did you become a priest?"

Frank was silent for a moment, remembering the time before the seminary, before the priesthood, when he was struggling the way Steve was struggling now.

"Because . . . at a certain point . . . I realized that that was the only thing that would really make me happy."

"That sounds crazy when you weigh it against all the other things, doesn't it?" Steve said.

"I guess, in a way, it does. But it's not written in stone that you have to be a priest, Steve."

"Do you think the church will ever let priests marry?"

"I wouldn't count on it. And you know what? I'm not sure they should."

"Why the hell not?"

"Because, in my better moments – and remember God is there in our worse moments too – but in my better moments what's going through my mind during the Mass is that, just as Christ did at the Last Supper, in a more profound way than I ever will, I am giving myself to these people as a priest. And celibacy is very much part of that sacrificial giving."

Steve said nothing for a while, just stared at the screen-saver on Frank's computer which was a stained-glass window. He seemed to be studying it.

"Is that Chartres or Notre Dame?" he asked.

"I think it's a window from the cathedral at Rouen. Ever been there?"

Steve shook his head. "Doesn't Rouen have something to do with Joan of Arc?"

"That's where they burned her at the stake," Frank said, leaning all the way back in his desk chair and choosing his next words carefully.

"Look, Steve, sometimes, if you just slow down, things become clearer. You calm the eagerness of either extreme, the eagerness to do something or to run away from it. I think God often calls a man to both marriage and the priesthood and leaves the choice up to that man. That's how I understand my own vocation. I wasn't called to celibacy and not called to marriage, but I was called to both and chose celibacy. If I didn't think I could have been happily married, celibacy would hardly be a sacrifice and sacrifice is what it's all about. Sacrifice for the Kingdom of God."

"Any regrets?"

"No . . ." Frank shook his head slowly, thinking

of his meeting with Joyce that afternoon. "Oh . . . I have good days and bad days, like everybody. But I'm still passionate about the priesthood. Maybe not as romantic about it as I was in the seminary, but just as passionate."

"Thanks buddy." Steve got up. "I'll leave you in peace."

"Go in peace yourself," Frank told him. "And call me if you need to talk some more. The more you wrestle with this now the better."

Frank had planned to work on his homily after Steve left but instead he wrote in his journal, and as he wrote he realized that there was more he should have told Steve. It was something that the saints like Joan of Arc knew and Father Frank was just beginning to figure out.

Lord, every time someone says to me, 'you priests should be allowed to marry' what they're really saying is, 'I don't value the sacrifice you're making.' That hurts. That's where the real pain is.

The whole idea of sacrifice for the Kingdom of God is nonsense to the world. Look at Joan of Arc, look at St. Francis, look at Thomas More. What a waste, what a stupid thing they were doing is how it looked to most people. And Your crucifixion? Even your disciples didn't understand that one, a sacrifice that people mocked or were revolted by.

I think the priesthood is a kind of slow crucifixion. Not only giving up of sex, but giving up of the whole self to be used by You.

The doorbell rang. One long insistent ring.

Is this what Steve's afraid of Lord? Comfort him, guide him . . .

Another long ring. Ruthie began to bark from upstairs.

"Damn!" Frank went out into the hall and grabbed open the door. A third ring would surely wake Father O'Donnell.

Outside on the front stoop was George, in his rumpled tweed coat, hat in hand, stone cold sober.

"I want my ashes, Father," he said.

"I'm sorry, George, they're all gone." Frank said.

"All gone?"

"You'd better get home now. Patty's been worrying about you all day. I missed you at church." Frank walked him down the front steps.

"You missed me?"

"Sure. I know you like your ashes on Ash Wednesday."

"Next year, maybe."

"Don't wait 'til next year, George. Come to Mass on Sunday," Frank told him. "God missed you too."

Chapter Five:

Easter Vigil

BY THE BEGINNING OF MARCH, FRANK KNEW it was time to get serious about his running. Four months had passed since he'd clicked on his TV one Sunday afternoon, caught the finish of the New York City Marathon, and, to his surprise, pictured himself in that crowd of runners next year.

Frank had always exercised pretty regularly but the only race he'd ever run was a 5K. He'd finished 2nd in his age group at 23:35 and 7th overall, so the marathon fantasy didn't come completely out of the blue. Still, it was a long long way from 5 kilometers to 26.2 miles.

The next time Frank saw Chris at the Y he asked him about a 10K. Did he know a good one?

"There's the St. Paddy's Day 10K," Christopher told him. "You can get a registration form at the front desk. Already sent mine in."

"Perfect."

Frank had two weeks to beef up his training. Speed, not distance was his focus and there was only one way to increase speed – interval work that alternated high-speed running with slower jogs. And for intervals he had to get off the river road and onto a track.

He found a track behind the high school near the mall. He had to get up earlier to drive there but at 7 in the morning there was enough light and few enough other runners to get a good workout. His goal was to run 6 to 8 1:45 intervals around the quarter mile track alternating with recovery laps at 2:15. This would put him in pretty good shape for a competitive 10K, but he would have to build up to it.

Three times a week for the next two weeks Frank's day began by running round and round the track in his gray sweat pants and hooded PATRIOT'S sweatshirt. Sometimes he reversed direction, from counter-clockwise to clockwise, just to keep from going crazy.

The St. Paddy's Day 10K started and finished in front of Children's Hospital because the money raised by the race would help to build their new wing. Frank knew the place well from hospital visits with injured children and their frantic parents, but this was the first time he'd ever stood outside the front portico wearing a bright green t-shirt with a large black shamrock in a sea of hundreds of other t-shirted, shamrocked runners. Frank spotted Chris' red bandanna in the crowd and saw Eliot from the St. Anne's R.C.I.A. class.

At 9:30 on March 17 a large gong was struck – the hospital administration had vetoed a starting gun – and the race began.

Frank was one of the last runners to go through the gate, but by the half-way marker he had moved up towards the center of the pack running through the cordoned-off streets of the town. He pushed himself hard, imagining that he was going round and round the high school track where he'd trained.

Frank prayed to the rhythm of his feet, *Hail Mary full of Grace, the Lord is with thee. Blessed art Thou among women and blessed is the fruit of thy womb, Jesus.* He overtook more runners. *Holy Mary, Mother of God, pray for us sinners, now and at the hour of our death. Amen*

Finally, Father Frank saw the green plastic banner that marked the finish line ahead, and found he had one more high-speed spurt left in him. He was exhausted when he crossed the finish line, but he was satisfied. He'd run his first 10K in 45 minutes: 52 seconds. He'd hoped for 45 flat, but he knew taking more time for training would come at the expense of his parish duties which were his first priority.

Not bad, he told himself as he walked the kinks

out of his legs and stretched. Maybe in eight months he'd be ready for the marathon.

Maybe.

In the refreshment tent afterwards, Frank found Eliot who was drinking a huge plastic cup full of green beer.

"Looks good!" Frank said.

"I thought you gave up drinking for Lent, Father Frank," Eliot said, handing him one.

"Except for green beer. I got a Papal dispensation for green beer," Frank drank the beer quickly and reached for another. He felt as though he would never be able to quench his thirst.

Eliot teased him about it when the R.C.I.A. class met the following Wednesday night. "That was such an unpuritanical thing you did, Father."

"What?"

"Cutting yourself some slack for the beer after the race. A puritan wouldn't have, you know."

"Hey Eliot, Catholics aren't puritans. R.C.I.A. lesson #1."

"I'm finally figuring that one out," Eliot said. "From the outside all religious people sort of look alike."

A ripple of laughter went around the group sitting at the vast wooden table in the teachers' room at St.

Anne's school. The class had been meeting weekly since September and would end with confirmation at the Easter Vigil which was now ten days away.

R.C.I.A. stood for the Rite of Christian Initiation for Adults, an ancient rite that the Catholic Church had revived in the 1980's to deal with the growing number of converts.

There were twenty-eight people in the group this year – a "personal best" for Frank – people who lived within the parish borders but hadn't belonged to the church. Some were lapsed Catholics, others frustrated Protestants, and still others, like Eliot, were curious agnostics. All had heard the bells of St. Anne's and found their way to Father Frank.

Tonight Frank was explaining "Pascal's Wager." Blaise Pascal, the French philosopher, had said that nobody could prove there was an afterlife and nobody could prove there wasn't.

"So," Frank told the class, "it comes to a 50/50 bet. Any good gambler will tell you that if you have a 50/50 bet and on the one hand there is a very limited payoff of some happiness in this life, and on the other hand there is eternity with God in heaven, you have to go with the higher stakes, eternity with God. If you can't accept faith for any other reason, look at it as a gamble."

The class laughed again.

"And if you're going to gamble, get it right."

"Is that all there is to it?" Eliot wanted to know. His expression was serious now, and his brown eyes behind his glasses searched Frank's face.

"No," Frank admitted. "The paradox of Pascal's Wager is that if that's how you approach faith, you're only deluding yourself. Christ himself sets the bar much higher for all of us."

The class groaned.

"But," Frank paused and made a gesture with his hands as if he were shoving a great pile of money into the center of the table, "if I didn't believe in the eternity-with-God part," he asked, "would I be doing what I'm doing on earth?"

The room grew silent. Nobody could deny that Frank's very priesthood witnessed to how much he had staked on Pascal's Wager.

The first R.C.I.A. class was always the most awkward, the most difficult, the one that people approached the most tentatively, as if they already had one foot out the door. So back in September Frank had tried to put them at ease.

He had stood at the blackboard, chalk in hand, and said, "Okay, tell me all the *negative* impressions you have of the Catholic Church."

The ice was broken and the class responded, timidly

at first, and then with increasing assertiveness. Frank wrote it all down.

"It seems like Catholics worship the Virgin Mary as much as Jesus."

"Some Catholics go to confession just so they can go out and sin again."

"They're such hypocrites, they're not supposed to use birth-control but everyone knows they do."

"You're tools of the Pope because you think he's infallible, but he's human too."

"The Catholic Church hates women!"

"Any more?" He held his piece of chalk poised.

"You think your religion is better than anyone else's." Frank wrote that one down too.

"More?"

No more.

Frank joined them around the table and turned to look back at the list on the blackboard.

"Let's deal with issue #4 – Papal infallibility – right now. We don't have time to go into all the others tonight, but we'll talk about each and every one of these issues, without any ducking or waffling or sugar-coating between now and Easter. And you'll probably think of more as we go along."

"Papal infallibility was established by a Papal Bull in 1870. The principle is that *only* when the Pope asserts that he is speaking infallibly on faith and morals is he infallible. Okay, you might say, he can do that anytime he wants, can't he? Well yes, in principle, but it hasn't worked out quite that way. In fact, the only time in history it has actually been invoked after that was in 1950, when Pope Pius XII asserted infallibly that the Virgin Mary was assumed bodily into Heaven, which is Catholic doctrine."

"You're kidding," Eliot said. "You mean that all those Popes in the Middle Ages who behaved so badly weren't acting infallibly?"

"No, that was all too human. The infallible part of their office wasn't affected by their sin."

"Amazing! That's one of the world's biggest hang-ups with Catholicism."

"You're right," Frank admitted. "I don't know how the concept got so bent out of shape, but now, I'd like you to put all negatives aside for the moment and focus on what it was that brought you to this class today. Something brought you here today, some nudge, some strange attraction."

He looked around at the group.

"Maybe you've always hated institutional religion. You've seen plenty of hypocrites who go to church on Sundays and then seem to behave as badly as anyone else, maybe worse. If that's Christianity, you can do without it . . . and yet there is a nagging sense of spiritual drift as you grow older. There must be more to life . . . this can't be all there is . . . so you begin to search and, to your surprise, and the surprise of your family and friends, you end up here."

"Or maybe you're already a Christian but the beliefs of the denomination you were baptized into have become so watered down that church feels more like a town meeting, or a social organization, than a religious service, and at least the Catholics have kept some of those nice old mysterious rituals."

"Or maybe you were born and raised a Catholic but had the usual run-ins with overly strict nuns or harsh priests (they're human too, I can vouch for that), but now you're getting older and those childhood hurts have eased. Whatever the nuns or priests did or didn't do to you in grade school doesn't seem as important as finding an adult faith you can live by. And die by. Dying with the sacraments beats dying without them," he added, "because you die at peace. Nobody every regrets dying a Catholic."

Father Frank walked back to the blackboard, and next to his list of criticisms wrote down an algebraic equation: $F/D = ?$

The class looked at him blankly.

"F stands for faith, D for doubt. I'm asking you to think about your faith/doubt ratio between now and Easter. This will tell you where you are spiritually at this point, and it will change as we move through the course."

"Why such a mathematical way of looking at matters of the spirit? Because, I've learned by experience,"

Frank grimaced, "many people can have a very high faith-to-doubt ratio and still believe themselves to be *unbelievers,* because the devil sits heavily on the doubt side of the scale. I'm not insisting on a hairy devil with horns and hooves but the devil of negativity and pride, especially pride, which can skew your faith."

"If you're like most people, you probably have a lot more faith than you realize. Be open to this during the R.C.I.A. course. Try not to focus so hard on those doubts the devil magnifies."

Just then, the wall clock gave off a loud BUZZ. A few people around the table jumped, including Frank.

"Talking of the devil will do that every time," he'd laughed.

Now, six months later, Frank was preparing the class for the final hurdle before being confirmed at the Easter Vigil: confession. For most, it would be the first time they'd entered one of those mysterious boxes at the back of the church to bare their souls.

"How long will you have, Father Frank?" Eliot asked. "Do you want to know about my *whole life?*"

"As much as you need."

Frank felt their nervousness, so he explained the intricacies of the confessional to help allay their fears.

At St. Anne's, as in most Catholic churches, there

were two kinds: the smaller, old fashioned curtained-off kind with kneelers and a screen between confessor and penitent; and the larger reconciliation rooms with a proper door. Inside these rooms was also a kneeler and a screen, as well as a partition which you could walk around and sit down and confess to the priest face to face.

Both confessionals had a system of lights on the outside, red for occupied, green for free. This was so you didn't barge in on another person in the middle of confession.

"If we kneel behind a screen, do you really not know who we are?" someone asked.

"People always wonder about that," Frank answered. "Sometimes I do and sometimes I don't."

"But if you do, do you pretend you don't?"

Frank nodded. "I always act as though it were a total stranger because the person is seeking anonymity by choosing to kneel before the screen rather than confess face to face. Different priests may handle this differently, but if someone comes to me behind the screen I'm not going to embarrass that person by acknowledging them. And very often I don't know. It surprises people sometimes but you can't imagine how many voices a priest hears, and also people usually speak in a more hushed tone, and we *really* can't see them. So we're not as sure as people sometimes think we are."

"What should we confess? What if we haven't

committed some great hot sin? What do you look for in a confession?"

"I try to listen hard to see what sin is bothering the person the most."

"So that's what you address?"

"Not just *address,* because we're not just counselors. What we *forgive,* and it's not my forgiving, it's God's. I'm just a channel for God's forgiveness. I don't mean that I'm not somehow in a human way forgiving the person as well but that's not the issue. It's God forgiving the person. That was drilled into us in the seminary; don't be stingy with God's forgiveness. The first rule of the confessional for the priest, after absolute confidentiality of course, is to be kind. And the second rule is be kind. And the third rule is be kind . . . ."

"Even if it's a sin like abortion?"

"Yes," he said, "if there's true repentance."

Back in his room that night Frank updated the runner's journal on his computer. After entering his running statistics, Frank's mind returned to the subject of confession.

I think as a priest I'm sometimes more concerned about the people who don't have a sense of sin in their lives than about the people who have

committed the big huge headline sins. I'm more worried about those who don't come to confession at all, don't even know it exists or would apply to them, like the Pharisees.

The Pharisees in the Bible got a lot of bad press because they were compared to Jesus. Who are the Pharisees today? They're the establishment, the movers and shakers of society. Respectable, looked up to. But the problem is still the same: they don't know their own sinfulness. Have no sense of it at all, like the Pharisees who thought the real sinners are the low lifes, the prostitutes and tax collectors, who hung around with Jesus.

The irony is, the Pharisees received the harshest criticism by Jesus of any group. That was because of the hardness of their hearts. They thought only other people needed God's forgiveness, not them. Still do.

During the next week, all the members of the R.C.I.A. went to confession and received absolution. Father O'Donnell heard Frank's confession and then he himself confessed to another priest in the diocese.

"A regular spiritual spring cleaning," he joked to Frank.

At midnight on the Saturday before Easter, Father Frank was standing next to the small bonfire which had been set up on the pavement in front of St. Anne's. It was a cold, gusty night and Frank's vestments whipped in the wind as he lit the fire and made the sign of the cross over it. With him were the twenty-eight members of the R.C.I.A. class who were officially known as *catechumens,* from the Greek word for "instructed ones."

Dear Friends in Christ, he prayed outloud, *on this most holy night, when our Lord Jesus Christ passed from death to life, the Church invites her children throughout the world to come together in vigil and prayer. This is the Passover of the Lord: if we honor the memory of His death and resurrection by hearing His word and celebrating His mysteries, then we may be confident that we shall share His victory over death and live with Him for ever in God.*

Frank took the heavy Easter candle and, before lighting it, cut a cross on it with a small knife, then traced the Greek letter alpha above the cross and the Greek letter omega below it. Then he inserted five grains of incense, which represented the five wounds of Christ, into the cross he had carved on the candle and lit the candle from the bonfire.

Christ our Light! he sang out in a rich baritone. *Thanks be to God!* the group around him responded. Then, lifting the great candle high Father Frank led the catechumens into the darkened church.

In the open doorway he sang a second time: *Christ*

our Light! The crowd of parishioners waiting inside responded *Thanks be to God!* as he entered. He walked slowly down the center aisle, stopping three times to pass the flame to the people at the end of the pews who caught the light with their own small candles and passed it along to the others. Frank then proceeded all the way to the altar, where he turned and lifted the Easter candle for the third time. By now St. Anne's was aglow.

Christ our Light! Frank sang out once more. *Thanks be to God!* the congregation responded even more enthusiastically the third time. Slowly the church lights came on and the most joyous celebration of the Christian year began.

After the readings and the homily it was time for the sacraments of initiation. Any catechumen who had never been baptized was now baptized and then joined the others in front of the altar. Frank stood facing them and the congregation in the pews.

"My dear candidates for confirmation," he addressed the members of the R.C.I.A. class, and lifted his hands and held them outstretched over the group as he prayed:

"All powerful God, Father of our Lord Jesus Christ
by water and the Holy Spirit
You freed Your sons and daughters from sin
and gave them new life.

Send Your Holy Spirit upon them
to be their helper and guide.

Give them the spirit of wisdom and understanding,
the spirit of right judgment and courage,
the spirit of knowledge and reverence.
Fill them with the spirit of wonder and awe in
Your presence.
We ask this through Christ our Lord."

Father Frank moved slowly down the line of catechumens. They were all there. He had lost none of them. He called each one by name, anointed each one with oil, and said to each one as he did so, "Be sealed with the Gift of the Holy Spirit." Their eyes were shining, and by the time he reached the end of the line Frank's eyes were shining too.

Of all the joys of his priesthood, the greatest joy was seeing the light go on in another person and knowing he had been the instrument of God to bring about that light. Hardness of heart had melted, and in its place were a new joy and a new peace. Each time that happened, Frank felt like a man experiencing the Divine for the very first time.

Chapter Six:

Good Shepherd

A FEW WEEKS AFTER EASTER, FRANK WAS sitting in his office agonizing over his homily for Good Shepherd Sunday. He'd been working on it for more that an hour and still hadn't come up with anything worth saying. Writing a homily wasn't just cranking out a speech; a priest was supposed to prayerfully reflect on the life of the parish in the light of the special challenges it was facing, and preach to that, using one of the readings assigned for the day. Frank never found it easy, but usually it wasn't this hard either.

One reason Frank was getting nowhere this morning was that he was constantly being interrupted. Unlike Protestant ministers who were granted time-out when they were working on their Sunday sermon, Catholic priests were expected to be perpetually available.

The latest phone call came from St. Anne's school where the first graders needed Father Frank right away.

"Can't Father O'Donnell go?" he asked Evelyn, the parish secretary, when she buzzed him on the intercom?

"They want *you*."

Frank had worked hard for the past two years at being wanted by everyone at St. Anne's, but today their endless demands were getting on his nerves.

"Is it an emergency?"

"Not unless you consider a lot of six year olds crawling around a classroom on all fours bleating an emergency."

"BLEEDING?"

"No, *bleating*, with a t."

"Okay," he sighed. "Okay!" He clicked DON'T SAVE on the screen and shut down his computer. He'd have to start all over again when he got back.

Once outside Father Frank's mood lifted because it was one of those glorious spring days when his senses felt like they'd crawled out of a cave after a long winter's sleep. He could smell the fragrance of a lilac bush that he hadn't even known was in bloom, and the silky white petal of a dogwood blossom brushed his cheek as he walked down the path towards the school.

He stopped and pulled the branch toward him to see the markings on the petals, believed, in olden times, to be the wounds of Christ. A pair of blue jays flew out of the dogwood and soared to the top of another, where they jabbered at him until he let the branch go.

"Lord, You really are a marvel in the spring!" Frank thought.

A verse from St. John's Gospel floated into his mind: *I am come that they might have life, and have it more abundantly.*

That was John 10:10, which came right before the Good Shepherd passage in the Bible. Maybe he could work that into his homily, after he got the first grade straightened out.

Frank expected to be accosted by a lot of noise when he entered the school but the only sounds he heard were the usual murmurings of voices coming through the classroom doors opening onto the hall. From the first grade classroom came a loud, "Hush! Here he comes."

When he stepped inside the room Frank saw at once the source of all the excitement. Six small desks had been pushed together in the center of the room to form a kind of altar, and draped over them was a white sheet painted on the sides with different sized sheep grazing in a beautiful meadow, under the smiling eyes of a tall man wearing a beard and a brown bathrobe.

Frank pointed to the man and asked the children, standing in squirmy silence around their masterpiece, "Who's this?"

"JESUS!"

"And who are these?" Frank gestured towards the sheep.

"The first grade!"

"It's wonderful," he laughed. "It's just wonderful. I'll put it on the altar on Sunday so the real Good Shepherd can get a good look at it."

"Here's me, Father Frank," said a girl with red hair. She was Kim, Patty's daughter. "I'm the sheep in the party shoes."

"Sure," he nodded. "I can tell that's you."

He walked around the altar cloth, inspecting each sheep carefully. One was wearing a baseball cap backwards, another had on a blue striped t-shirt, and still another with only three legs — "You can't see the other one, but it's there," the artist said — had a large purple bow on the top of her head.

"Now let's see," Frank said. "If I were going to draw my sheep, I think I'd put him in a pair of Nikes. Actually, he'd need two pairs, wouldn't he?"

"You can't be a *sheep*, Father Frank," Kim told him firmly. "You have to be a Good Shepherd."

And suddenly Frank realized that he was looking at his homily for Sunday.

The Pope had designated Good Shepherd Sunday as a World Day of Prayer for Vocations, a day for the whole Church to pray for Christian vocations to the priesthood and the religious life. The Holy Father had stated that the vocations were always out there because God had promised He would always provide shepherds for his sheep.

But the problem was that today too many people identified with the sheep rather than with the shepherd, as even Frank had just done. The demands and distractions of modern life made it hard to hear, or answer, God's radical call to be a shepherd to His sheep. Frank would use the first grade altar cloth to make this point in his homily.

When he returned to the rectory he found Evelyn hard at work assembling the new parish directory. She really was indispensable, he thought.

But sometimes Frank wondered why Evelyn stayed. Her husband had retired, and all but one of her children were grown and on their own. The youngest, Jeff, was in junior high and a member of the Youth Group at St. Anne's.

Maybe it was Jeff who kept her involved. She could work and keep an eye on him at the same time. Junior high was a dangerous age.

"You look a lot more cheerful," she remarked as he walked back into the rectory.

"I am," said Frank. "And if I can just get thirty uninterrupted minutes at my computer, I'll be cheerful for the rest of the day."

But soon the phone rang again, and this interruption would not only ruin Frank's cheerfulness, but was to have consequences so painful that they would shake Frank's very faith in himself as a priest.

"That was Joyce," Evelyn buzzed Frank. "She's on her way over to update you on the Youth Retreat."

Frank had seen very little of Joyce since they'd last met in February so now he took out his notes from that meeting and reviewed them:

YOUTH RETREAT

WHEN: JUNE 6 and 7

THEME: "Let us build the City of God" ??????????????

FORMAT: Talk show !!!!!!!!!!!!!

Where do the sacraments come in?

When is the Mass?

What's my role if she decides not to have a Mass?

Can I participate without insisting on doing it my way?

What does God want here?

Frank sighed as he remembered his Ash Wednesday meeting with Joyce. Why hadn't he followed up on his suggestions to her? There were certainly ways to bring about compromise, but he'd been too busy with everything else.

Why hadn't he dropped in on the Youth Group meeting and explained to the kids why it was important to have a Mass at the Retreat? Why hadn't he taken time to hang out with the teenagers afterwards, maybe gone over to the gym and played some basketball with them, so they would know that he was a real person, and not a "plastic priest"?

Why had Joyce said that anyway? Frank felt the hurt of it all over again as he waited for her to arrive, and the longer she took to get there the more angry and defensive he became.

After fifteen minutes passed with no sign of Joyce he pounded the wall with his fist and turned his computer back on. He had just created a new document called "Good Shepherd Homily" when Joyce walked in carrying a pile of yellow papers.

"Wait 'til you see these, Father. They came out beautifully."

"What are they?" He hated the way his voice sounded already.

"The programs for the Retreat. Here's one for you."

She handed him a folded sheet of yellow paper and turned as if to go.

"Hold on, Joyce," Frank said, and gestured toward the chair on the other side of his desk. "I thought we were going to discuss this some more before your finalized things."

"Of course, Father," She sat on the edge of the chair and smiled at him. "It's pretty straight forward, actually. You host the first 'talk show,' I host the second, then the kids will break up into small groups which will probably go on and on and we'll come back together after breakfast the next day with a ratings game and a wrap-up."

"Ratings game?"

"You were in TV, weren't you Father?"

"A long time ago."

"Then you should know what ratings are." She uncrossed and recrossed her short legs. "In this case it will be sort of instant feedback from the kids. More sharing, really."

"And the Mass?"

She frowned. "The return bus is scheduled to leave the Retreat Center at 10:30. It's a long ride back and we promised the parents we'd have them home by lunch time."

"So, no Mass."

She shook her head.

"Then I'm sorry but I won't participate." He tossed his program back across the desk.

"But, who's going to host the first talk show?"

She was out of her chair now, standing squarely in the middle of his office with her hands on her hips.

"You'll just have to host them both, Joyce." Frank told her. "That way you're guaranteed to win the ratings game."

With that, Frank spun around in his chair and began to work furiously on his homily again.

He heard her gather up her pile of yellow programs and leave his office. Was there some hesitancy in her step? He couldn't tell.

He heard her say hello to Evelyn who was apparently just coming back in the front door.

"Hi, Joyce," he could hear Evelyn say. "Jeff's excited about the Retreat. Did you and Father get it all worked out?" But he couldn't hear Joyce's reply.

At a quarter to eleven, Frank remembered the nursing home; he was due to celebrate Mass there in fifteen minutes. Grabbing his Mass kit and the briefcase with his vestments in it, he rushed out of the rectory and jumped into his car.

As he got in, he knocked his right knee on the steering-wheel shaft. Damn, that was the knee he was trying to protect. Ever since the St. Patrick's Day race it had been bothering him, not all the time but more and more during his weekly long runs.

He was up to 30 miles a week now, five miles four times a week and ten miles on his day off, which usually ended with a session of icing his knee and resting it outstretched for an hour or two.

Maybe he should get a knee brace, or try heat instead of ice, or see a sports doctor because it wasn't getting any better and this latest bump wouldn't help. Frank hadn't made up his mind what to do about his knee by the time he pulled into the driveway of the nursing home, but he got out of the car very, very carefully.

The first person he saw in the TV room where they held the Mass was Mrs. Abernathy, who had just moved in to the home. She was sitting in a wheelchair, in her Christmas bathrobe, waiting for him.

"Are you bringing us Jesus, Father Frank?" she asked.

"Indeed I am, Mrs. A.," Frank laughed and began to set up for Mass.

They had arranged a table for him at one end of the room and about a dozen people were seated in chairs or wheelchairs facing the table. Frank opened the wooden case he had brought with him and took out various cloths and utensils while the members of the group chatted, dozed, or looked with interest.

First he spread a cloth, called a corporal, on the table, and then placed a silver chalice for the wine, and a silver paten for the bread on the cloth. He took out two beeswax candles and set them on either side, lit them, and then placed a brass crucifix in front, facing out towards the room. He put the still unconsecrated bread and wine to one side, to be ready when he needed them, and slipped out into the hallway to put on his vestments.

One of the nurses who assisted with the Mass played some music to quiet the chatterers down and wake the sleepers up. Then Frank entered the room again and stood behind the table.

"The Lord be with you," he said.

"And also with you," they answered.

"The Lord has risen and we are joyful and yet we are conscious of our sin and our need for forgiveness. Let us ask His mercy for our sins."

The nursing home residents bowed their heads.

Lord Jesus, You raise us to new life, Frank prayed.
Lord have mercy.
Lord Jesus, You forgive us our sins.
Christ have mercy.
Lord Jesus, You feed us with Your body and blood.
Lord have mercy.
May Almighty God have mercy on us and bring us to everlasting life. Amen.

He led them through the readings for the day and the responsorial psalm, which some responded to and some didn't. Then he stepped to one side and gave a little homily.

Most of these people had been members of St. Anne's for a long time, so he tried to tie them in to the parish whenever and however he could. Today he told them about the first graders and their Good Shepherd altar cloth.

"Now you may think that you can no longer help out at the church by arranging flowers, or ushering at Mass, or doing any of the special things you used to do. Sometimes you may feel frustrated because of this, but I want you to know that we still need you very much at St. Anne's. As a matter of fact the job we have for you is probably the most important job of all: we need you to pray."

"As one of my spiritual books says, 'Prayer changes all. Prayer recreates. Prayer is irresistible . . . One day when we are face to face with God and learn how marvelously our prayers have been answered, we will deeply, deeply regret how little we prayed in this life.'"

"I pray for you everyday," Mrs. Abernathy called out.

"So do I," another woman said. "I pray for you twice a day."

"Thank you," Frank said, with a lump in his throat. "I need your prayers, all priests do. We can't do it without your prayers."

"Well, I pray for the Brooklyn Dodgers," said an old man loudly. He had been dozing in the back of the room but now he was wide awake. The women turned to hush him up, but Frank came to his rescue.

"I pray for the Patriots, but it doesn't always help," he said. "Maybe more people are praying for the other team. Anyway, please keep up all your prayers. We love you and thank you for them."

Now Frank stood behind the altar he had created on the TV table, and began the most solemn part of the Mass. The room quieted down as he spoke the familiar words.

Father, You so loved the world that in the fullness of time You sent Your only Son to be our Savior. He was conceived through the power of the Holy Spirit, born of the Virgin Mary, a man like us in all things but sin. To the poor He proclaimed the good news of salvation, to prisoners, freedom, to those in sorrow, joy.

In fulfillment of Your will He gave Himself up to death, but by rising from the dead He destroyed death and restored life. That we might live no longer for ourselves He sent the Holy Spirit from You Father as His first gift to those who believe, to complete His work on earth and bring us the fullness of grace.

Frank held both hands over the chalice into which he had poured the wine, and the silver paten with the bread.

Father, may the Holy Spirit sanctify these offerings, let them become the body and blood of Jesus Christ our Lord as we celebrate the great mystery which He left us as an everlasting covenant. He always loved those who were His own in the world, when the time came for Him to be glorified by you, His Heavenly Father, He showed the depth of his love.

While they were at supper Jesus took bread, said the blessing, gave it to his disciples and said, "Take this all of you and eat it. This is my body which will be given up for you."

When the supper was ended He took the cup. Again, He gave You thanks and praise and gave the cup to His disciples and said, "Take this, all of you, and drink from it, this is the cup of my blood, the blood of the new and everlasting covenant. It will be shed for you and for all so sins may be forgiven. Do this in memory of me."

Because they couldn't come up to receive communion, Father Frank took it to them. He walked slowly around the room giving everyone a piece of consecrated bread, but he didn't distribute the consecrated wine for fear that it would interact with their medications.

Frank was always moved by the reverence he saw on the faces of the nursing home residents when they received the Body of Christ in their gnarled hands or on their tongues. It was a reverence that was neither young nor old but timeless and pure, and it never failed to bring him peace.

Chapter Seven:

Ordinary Time

JUNE WAS WEDDING MONTH. Frank struggled hard to satisfy brides who had been poring over bridal magazines since they were little girls. All too often their concept of the perfect wedding was a gauzy series of photo opportunities in a church setting. What they wanted from a priest was for him to stand there in his vestments and look official and benign, which made Frank feel like a commodity.

It was a dance. They tried to see how little they could do and still get married by a priest and Frank tried to inspire and attract them to the beauty of the marriage sacrament in which he believed so stongly.

At times he worried that he pushed too hard. Was he friendly enough? Was he fair? Did he blow it? Several brides simply took off and found another priest who would let them have their way.

Frank could understand why some older priests said they'd rather do ten funerals than one wedding, but the priests he really admired were the ones who had been at it twenty or thirty years and had not become cynical, the extraordinary ones who had kept their feelings for the liturgy and the priesthood so fresh that each time they performed a wedding they were truly channels for God's love and everyone could feel it.

Brenda was getting married and today was the wedding rehearsal at St. Anne's. She had given up trying to lure Frank out of the priesthood, and had become engaged to her old boyfriend on New Year's Eve. But she still wanted Frank to officiate.

He had just walked Brenda, her fiance and their attendants through the ceremony when his cell phone rang. He excused himself and stepped into the sacristy. When he came back his face was ashen.

"There's an emergency . . . one of the eighth graders . . . ." He looked over at Brenda who was sitting in the front pew with her parents and her bridesmaids.

"Do you have a pretty good idea about tomorrow?" he asked her. "I've got to get to the hospital." She nodded her frizzy blond head and Frank felt they'd come a long way in their relationship. He belonged to everyone in the parish and she'd finally accepted that.

"Okay," he said, and his words were rushed. "I need the groomsmen here 45 minutes before the wedding begins, everyone else a half hour before. Any last minute questions?" He looked over at the groom-to-be who was slouched on the other side of the aisle with his group.

"No? Then see you all tomorrow, and don't stay out too late tonight."

They laughed nervously and he was gone.

The call had been from Evelyn. Her son Jeff had tried to commit suicide and was in a coma at Children's Hospital.

Twelve minutes later Frank parked his car in the hospital parking lot and hurried in the emergency room door. The first people he saw in the waiting room were some Youth Group members from St. Anne's.

They were sitting against the far wall, some crying, some just sitting, and when they saw Father Frank come in they rushed at him.

"Is he okay?"

"Why'd Jeff do it Father?"

"Can we see him?"

Frank didn't know the answer to any of their questions but the last one. Obviously the emergency room personnel were keeping the semi-hysterical teenagers away from Jeff, wherever he was now.

Frank's heart went out to the young people. When

he reached his arms around as many as he could there were tears in his eyes too.

"I'll find him and let you know how he is." He tried to smile reassuringly. "Sit back down now. Calm yourselves . . . and pray. That's what he and his family need right now: *prayer.* Does anyone have a rosary?"

No one did, so he took his out of his pants pocket and gave it to them. The smooth wooden beads felt warm and reassuring as he handed them to one of the girls.

Inside the emergency room they directed him to the 3rd flood where he found Evelyn and her husband behind a curtained off area in a semi-private room. Jeff was lying unconscious in the bed by the window.

"He's going to be fine, isn't he Father?" Evelyn told him. Her husband just stared at his comatose son.

"Let's go find a place where we can talk," said Frank, aware of the other patient in the next bed. He guided Evelyn by the elbow and her husband followed.

At the end of the hall there was an alcove with a potted plant and some beige plastic chairs. Evelyn's husband dropped into a chair and covered his face with his hands.

"What happened?" Frank asked Evelyn as they sat down opposite each other.

Her story came out in bits and pieces. Jeff was apparently hanging out with the others down at the bridge over the river. At least, that's where the taxi-cab driver saw them, or rather the ambulance that the cabby had called for.

"You said suicide on the phone. Could another kid have pushed him off the bridge?"

She shook her head.

"No, the cab driver said he was up there on his own and just jumped. The rest were down in the underpass. The cab driver saw the whole thing because he was parked along the side of the road eating his lunch. Did I tell you he saved Jeff's life?"

"Tell me." Frank moved his chair closer and took her hand in both of his. God, she's brave, he thought.

"He radioed for help, then jumped in and swam to where he'd seen Jeff go in and pulled him to shore. Jeff was unconscious when he surfaced. The doctor says he saved Jeff's life, but he won't wake up, Father . . ."

She put her arms around her husband, who was slumped down in his chair, apparently lost in his own thoughts. With her tear-stained cheek resting on the top of her husband's bald spot, Evelyn looked up at Frank. "It can take days sometimes, the doctor says."

But in Jeff's case, it didn't. He was conscious by the next morning and ready to talk with Father Frank the next afternoon. The other patient had left so they had the hospital room to themselves.

"Hi," Jeff said softly from his bed. He looked worried and pale but he was wide-awake. He told Frank that he guessed he'd been upset ever since the Youth Retreat.

"I liked the Retreat," Jeff said. "It was cool to open up and cry with the other kids. But after we went back to school everything changed." Jeff gazed out the window and began to bite his fingernails.

Frank waited. When Jeff spoke again his voice was barely a whisper. "That's when the teasing started . . . some of the kids told other kids stuff that they'd heard at the Retreat . . . some of it was about me."

Inevitable, Frank thought angrily, absolutely inevitable. When you start messing around with the human heart without God there, you make people bleed without a Healer present.

"Is that what made you do what you did, Jeff?" he asked. "It that what made you jump?"

"Yeah," Jeff mumbled. "I guess so." He bit his fingernails some more and then began to talk again.

"But, you know, it was something else too, Father," He seemed to be struggling to express a deeper problem.

"Teasing's not really such a big deal. I do it to other people too . . . You know what I think was the worst thing after the Retreat?"

"What."

"It was going back to the same boring everyday shit . . ."

"Like what?" Frank asked.

"Oh," Jeff looked at the ceiling. "Like boring classes and homework and getting behind in math, and science which I hate, and getting hassled by my parents to make good grades like my older brothers. Sometimes I think I can't stand another minute of it. Every day it's – time to get up, Jeff! – and the same shit starts all over again. I can't take it anymore . . ."

"Jeff," Frank smiled and stepped closer. "God is in the boring everyday shit, too. That's the secret, the great secret of life, and it changes everything."

Could a thirteen-year-old understand something that most of the world didn't?

"Jeff, have you ever heard of 'Ordinary Time'?"

"Maybe. There's something about it in that missal on the back of the pews, isn't there?"

"Yes," Frank leaned forward and looked into Jeff's eyes. "Ordinary Time is part of the church year. A big part. Actually, everything that isn't something special like Christmas, or Easter, or Lent, is called Ordinay Time. It's *most* of the time."

"So?"

"So, I can help you deal with it."

"How?"

"By a way that was invented by a French nun who wasn't much older than you are. St. Theresa called it the 'Little Way' and it works. What you do is include God in everything, in every hurt, in every pain, in everything that seems boring, in every moment when you feel you just can't stand what you have to do, and He'll transform them and give you peace."

Jeff looked skeptical and turned his head to stare out the window again.

"It's a kind of marathoner's mentality," Frank said, trying a different approach. "Each small step isn't that important but they can add up to something really big."

Frank got ready to leave. "It takes a while to practice the Little Way, so I want you to come see me whenever you get discouraged. Don't wait until you're really down. Come before that. Okay?"

Jeff shrugged.

"Do you know where my office is?"

Jeff nodded.

"Let's make a date right now," Frank pressed him. "How about next Sunday after Mass?"

"The kids'll see me go in."

"Right," Frank nodded. "Let's meet over at the gym. Shoot a few baskets. Okay?" Jeff said nothing as Frank headed towards the door.

But at the doorway, Father Frank turned back to the boy in the bed.

"Try St. Theresa's Little Way, Jeff. It's got to be better than jumping off of bridges, and scaring people who love you half to death."

As soon as Frank returned to the rectory he raced up the stairs and changed into his running clothes. He was out the front door before anyone knew he'd come, or gone.

He didn't wait for the green light on the corner of Route 1 but ran straight across it, dodging the cars.

"Stupid," he muttered when one almost hit him. Stupid . . . stupid . . . stupid, his legs seemed to accuse him as they pounded the pavement down towards the river road. His anger had moved from Joyce to himself, *Hail Mary full of grace,* he forced himself to pray, but his legs kept accusing him: stupid . . . stupid . . . . stupid. *Blessed art thou among women and blessed is the fruit of thy womb, Jesus.*

Frank's right knee burned with pain, but he kept running. Stupid . . . stupid . . . stupid. The pain spread to his left knee and he nearly fell. Finally, when he was in sight of the railway bridge, he stopped. Both legs were on fire now and he dragged himself back to St. Anne's in agony. That night he wrote only two lines in his runner's journal.

Ran less than a mile today. The weather? I didn't notice. My feelings? That I'm not worthy to call myself Your priest.

He stopped typing and rested his forehead on his clenched fists. All he could see in his mind's eye was the last sentence of his Ash Wednesday notes: What does God want here?

In his pride and anger at Joyce he'd completely ignored what God wanted to happen at the Retreat. Frank could have gone along and protected the kids, and if he'd gone Jeff might not have done what he did. The hardness of Frank's own heart was to blame for the near tragedy. Jeff was alive today only by the grace of God, and the courage of a cab driver.

Night prayer in the *LITURGY OF THE HOURS* was designed to help the person reading it let go of the hurt and disappointments of the day. – "Sufficient unto the day is the evil therein," Jesus had told his disciples, "Don't carry it forward to tomorrow." So night prayer always included a brief examination of conscience and a penitential prayer to clear away each day's pain.

Frank didn't need to examine his conscience very closely that night because his failure was foremost in his mind, so he turned quickly to the penitential prayer:

> *Father of mercy, like the prodigal son, I return to*
> *You and say:*
> *"I have sinned against You, and am no longer*
> *worthy to be*
> *Called Your son."*
>
> *Christ Jesus, Savior of the world, I pray with the*
> *repentant thief*

To *whom You Promised Paradise:*
"Lord, remember me in Your kingdom,"
Holy Spirit, fountain of love, I call on You with
trust:
"Purify my heart, and help me to walk as a child
of light."
                                        Amen

Frank finally slept that night, but as soon as he got out of bed the next morning he winced. Both knees throbbed with pain when he put weight on them. It was definitely time to see a doctor.

His regular doctor sent him to a sports therapist who gave him orthotics for his shoes, taught him exercises to do before and after running, and said that from now on Frank should restrict himself to fewer than three miles a day, and he'd have to build up slowly to that by walking first because it wasn't so hard on the knees. A marathon in November? Highly unlikely.

"Highly unlikely" . . . Frank mulled these words over and over as he walked Ruthie. Drop the "highly" and you were left with "unlikely" which wasn't so bad. It left the possibility open, Frank thought. The next day he received a fat envelope in the mail: his registration had been picked for the New York City Marathon.

He never walked down to the river road anymore,

but turned back into the town past the public swimming pool. He saw a lot of the St. Anne's kids there because as July progressed the heat began to sock in.

"Don't take Ruthie too far, Frank," Father O'Donnell warned him when the daily walks began. "I don't want her to collapse from heat exhaustion."

Ruthie was only Frank's on loan, to cheer him up while he couldn't run. One day, long ago, she had followed Father O'Donnell home to the rectory and he had named her after Ruth in the Bible. When Father O'Donnell retired from St. Anne's, Ruthie would follow him out.

As the days got hotter Father Frank's prayer life seemed to dry up too. He was faithful to his *LITURGY OF THE HOURS* and on days when he didn't have to celebrate Mass – St. Anne's had cut back for the summer – he would offer up a private Mass at a little altar he'd set up in his room.

Yet he felt further away from God than he ever had. Dry, like a man abandoned to scratch out his existence on parched earth. Still, he hung on desperately to this routine, waiting for Divine consolation, like rain, to water his soul.

He went to the pool every day, joked around with the kids, swam laps, and worked to get his body back in shape, hoping that his spirits would follow. Then one day, in the cool of an early morning, Frank went back to the track and began running again.

August brought psychological relief: two weeks of vacation. Frank found a new seminarian to help Father O'Donnell – Steve had been ordained in June and was now associate pastor of his first parish – so Frank left to visit his family and spend a week with friends at Cape Cod with a clear conscience, and a tremendous feeling of relief.

The first person he saw when he pulled in the driveway of his parents' house was his sister Claire. She was out on the front porch watching the twins who were crawling around in a small sea of toys. When she saw Frank she picked up one in each arm and ran to the car. "Where'd you get that horrible hat?" she asked as she kissed him and handed him little Frank. When he took the baby in his arms she snatched it off his head.

"Hey," he protested. "That's Dad's old fishing hat!"

"I knew I'd seen it before. Trouble with you priests is, you don't have wives to dress you properly."

"Or nag us." He shot back. They were laughing as they carried the babies and Frank's things into the house.

It was good to be home: to be fussed at by his sister and fussed over by his mother, to watch baseball on TV with his dad and brother-in-law. To see the change in the twins since Easter. They were starting to pull themselves up now. By Christmas, they'd be walking.

It went so fast, Frank thought. Life went by so fast when you measured it by the change in a child.

Remember this, he told himself, when you're back at St. Anne's.

On Sunday they all went to Mass together. The words they were saying, the prayers they were praying, the scriptures they were hearing read were exactly the same as those being said, and prayed, and read that day at St. Anne's. Not only at St. Anne's, but all over America and all over the world, in hundreds of different languages.

The old fishing hat was back on Frank's head when he pulled out of the driveway the next Sunday morning. It took him five hours to reach the Cape and another hour to check in with the rental agent, get the keys and find the cottage.

Frank was the first one to arrive so he aired the mattresses, shook the sand out of the throw rugs, and left a note for the others saying he'd gone out for beer and basics.

The four priests had taken a week's vacation together at the Cape since seminary. During the day they swam, lay on the beach, watched girls and kept each other honest. At night they played poker.

Frank needed to be with other men who were dealing with the same frustrations and temptations that he was. He'd learned, the hard way, not to try to face them without a support system.

His sin that first summer after ordination had been forgiven by God long ago, Frank knew, but it still haunted him whenever he was alone at the Cape. Even for a couple of hours.

He had been completely burned-out that summer five years ago, plus he had post-ordination depression and a feeling of spiritual exhaustion. Not that any of that excused what Frank did. Nothing excused it.

It had happened at the end of the vacation, after the others had gone. Frank's first pastor had generously given him a couple extra days off so he had stayed on at the cottage alone, reading, praying, and by the third day actively looking for company.

He found it in Cindy, a young woman with a beautiful tan and long blond hair, whom he'd noticed on the beach during the week. She smiled at him when he jogged by and again when he jogged back. He approached her and they started to talk. She motioned to the empty beach towel next to hers and he was tired enough, and lonely enough to lie down next to her.

What was so sexy about putting sun tan oil on someone's back? Frank wondered. It was an innocent touch of warm flesh on warm flesh, out in the open, entirely acceptable, but it had aroused him, and he'd seen arousal in her eyes too.

Frank could have walked away then, but he hadn't. They'd gone back to his cottage and made love. Wordlessly, because Frank couldn't remember the words that went with it.

She'd never known he was a priest, but he knew and after he'd taken her home, it had hit him with full force.

He'd been given certain gifts by God, in his looks and his personality, and these gifts had been given to draw people closer to God, not to Frank. If he had been doing what he was supposed to be doing, being a priest, he could have brought Cindy closer to God, and His love, and His joy, and His peace. Instead Frank had used her as a sex object.

Once back at the cottage that summer after ordination, Frank had realized he couldn't stay there another night. He'd frantically cleaned the place from top to bottom, praying for Cindy the whole time. After a couple of hours the house still seemed unfit for the next renters, but Frank was exhausted. So he'd thrown his things in his car and left.

When he got to Boston he went to a Catholic church, woke up the priest, told him that he needed to confess. It was then about midnight but the sleepy priest had willingly opened up the church, put on his stole and entered the confessional.

Frank had knelt before the screen and poured out his sin. The priest had listened carefully and then told him to go back to his parish and get on with his priesthood. Not to talk about it, or brag about it to other priests like some kind of conquest, because it wasn't. It was a betrayal. And never to do it again.

Then the priest had given Frank a penance and absolution, and told him God loved him, still and always.

Frank had asked one more favor as they stepped out of the confessional. Could he sleep in the church that night? The other priest seemed to understand.

"I'll have to lock you in," he'd said. Frank had nodded and walked to the door with him.

When he was alone Frank had stretched out in a wooden pew at the rear of the church. He didn't think he'd be able to sleep anywhere else that night than next to the Sacred Heart of Jesus.

Now, as Frank returned to the cottage after his shopping trip, he was enormously relieved to see other cars in the driveway. His friends had finally arrived. As he carried the beer and groceries in the back door, he heard someone shout out, "Okay! Tom Cruise is here . . . let the good times roll!"

And they did. During the day the four priests usually hung out together at the beach, for a while anyway, and then gradually separated to wind-surf, or fish, or dig for clams, or bike into town where there was a great second-hand bookstore.

And Frank ran, farther and farther each day.

They enjoyed each other's company, but each man also craved time alone after the incessant demands of parish life. They gathered together again for dinner. And every night there was poker on the round green table in the kitchen afterwards. Five card stud.

The last day they were at the Cape they woke up to sheeting rain so poker started up again after an early Mass and breakfast, and lasted all day and into the night.

Frank relished the competition of the game and the unceasing conversation that flowed around it.

"Who's dealer?" he asked as he poured himself a second cup of coffee and put down the sports pages. The rain pounded on the roof and coursed down the window panes.

"Who was last, last night?"

"Brian was, so it's your deal, Tom," Bill reached behind him for the cards. "Clear off the newspapers! Charlie, you in or out?

Charlie, who did all the cooking, was across the kitchen cleaning a blue fish.

"In. Think I want to stand here and listen to the three of you go at it? What's wild?"

"Deuces," Frank said as Charlie sat down to his left. Frank shuffled and dealt everyone two cards, one face down and one face up.

"Anyone hear that moaning sound in the attic last night? I kept hearing it," Brian said as he peeked at his face down card. He was showing a nine of diamonds face up.

"Something's been moaning up there all week," said Frank. "Obviously the place is haunted."

He had an eight of spades face up and a queen of hearts in the hole. The hand had potential, but this was just the beginning.

"Openers?" Frank looked across at Bill who was showing a jack of clubs, "You're high."

"I'm in for a buck," Bill said. "So what if the house is haunted? We're priests, we're friends of the dead, right?"

The others each put in a dollar and Frank dealt everyone another card, face up.

"Maybe we're living below purgatory, just sort of stumbled on it," Brian laughed.

"If this is it, it's not too bad."

"That's what I kept telling my R.C.I.A. class," said Frank. "They were very hung-up on purgatory, couldn't understand why Catholics insist on it when they couldn't find anything specific about it in their Bibles."

"So did you show them where it was?"

"Yea, I Corinthians 3:13"

"What about I Peter 1:7?"

"There too," Frank agreed. "Hey, let's get some betting going. You're high," he said to Brian who was now showing a nine and a deuce, giving him a pair of nines.

Brian looked at the ace that Frank had just been dealt and shoved three dollars into the pot. Frank and Bill matched him and Charlie folded.

"Oh, come on," Brian protested. "You never stick around. You've been the King of Fold all week."

"Sorry, too rich for my blood."

Frank dealt another round to the three still in the game. He didn't like the second wild card he'd just handed Brian on a silver platter, but the king of diamonds he'd dealt himself got his juices going. Anyway, Brian was bluffable.

"I told the class that purgatory's a kind of continuity between this life and the next." Frank said.

"I'll see your five and raise you two," he looked at Brian who had just added a five-dollar bill to the pot.

Now just Brian and Frank were in the game.

"I hear two dominant images of God when I talk to people," Bill said, flipping his cards face down and folding. "Even in my R.C.I.A. class. One: God's just a nice guy, who forgives everyone, and everything, no matter how you've lived your life. . ."

"The everyone-goes-to-heaven trap," Charlie interrupted him. "What a load of shit."

"But I hear the other one almost as often," Bill insisted. "God as a kind of cop who metes out punishment after death according to some long tally of violations He's been keeping on you, things you've forgotten ages ago. People seem to think Heaven or hell is up to God's memory, not His mercy."

"You know what bothers me most about both of them?" Frank asked. "They're both extrinsic because there's no real connection between this life and the next. That's where purgatory comes in. It connects them."

He really wanted to beat Brian who was hunkering down, elbows on the table, blue eyes shifting between Frank's hand and his own, but Frank was also fascinated by the discussion of purgatory.

"Time for beer," Charlie grabbed four cans out of the refrigerator. "Conversation's getting really heavy." All four paused a minute to concentrate on the beer.

"Let me tell you where I ended up with the R.C.I.A.," Frank said.

Brian groaned. "Are we playing poker or what?"

Frank reached over and dealt Brian the three of spades, and then the king of clubs to himself. Brian's hand was obviously better but he didn't know what Frank had in the hole, so Frank decided to let him sweat it out and matched Brian's next bet too.

"Purgatory's a good place," said Bill, "because there's a clarity about your relationship with God there."

"Right!" Frank nodded vehemently. "You know you've been forgiven, you know you're on your way to heaven, but you have to be transformed first because your sins have distorted your soul. Sure, there's got to be some suffering in purgatory because that's where the hardness of heart is peeled away and you stand in full realization of how far you are from God."

"That's why we're all going to spend a lot of time there," Charlie said. "Maybe saints go straight to heaven . . ."

"But don't forget there's an overlap up there," Frank interrupted him.

"And a showdown right here," Brian said, flipping all his cards face up. "Three nines," he said. "Read 'em and weep, Tom. What ya got?"

"Two kings," said Frank softly, showing all his cards. He scooped up the pot money and rained it down on top of Brian's head.

"You win, Bri."

Frank was deeply moved when he celebrated his first Mass after vacation. As the parishioners of St. Anne's came forward to receive communion he was struck by the feeling that as a priest he'd come to know these people at a very deep level. I buried her husband, he thought, I visited *him* in the hospital, I married *their* daughter, I brought *them* into the church . . .

It was a wonderful feeling. The time away had given him a whole new perspective on both St. Anne's and his priesthood there.

St. Anne's was more than just a church, it was a neighborhood, a place where you belonged if you lived in a certain geographical area whether you knew it or not, whether you wanted to or not.

Frank had always been curious about "church shopping" Protestants. Just what were they shopping for? Someone in the pulpit to tell them what they wanted to hear, or who had a charismatic personality? And when that someone was transferred to another church did they follow him or continue where they were even though the reason they were there no longer existed?

Were they attracted to a beautiful building? It wasn't about buildings, Frank thought. He had been to some really homely Catholic churches where the spirit of love was so strong that they radiated beauty in spite of bad architecture and cheap furnishings.

Or were church shoppers looking for a church full of people who thought just the way they did? Maybe this was the result of American consumerism that had somehow become applied to churches.

It was kind of an Internet mentality. You're anonymous, you're not attached to any place, but you want a certain piece of information that only you define, and you go to a web site where people with that same special interest go. It's not connected to the messiness of real life.

The Catholic Church had been dealing with the messiness of real life for a long, long time. Your neighbors were the people you had to get along with every day and, according to Jesus: love. They were a group of people thrown together geographically and the size of a Catholic parish was usually large enough to give you an interesting mix. Most of all, there was a feeling of place, a feeling of belonging.

And what if your parish priest was transferred? So what? You might be relieved, or you might be sad, but that wasn't the point. The priest wasn't the point. Jesus was.

The priest and the Church were an imperfect means to deliver the perfect: God's love for His people manifested in the Eucharist.

September was a golden month at St. Anne's. The school started up again, the Mass schedule filled out and Frank felt energized by his vacation.

He sent away for a heart monitor he saw advertised in a runner's magazine. The "unlikely" became likely, and then definite, when he told Father O'Donnell that he needed to take Sunday, November 1st off.

"Oh you do, do you?" Father O'Donnell was not pleased. "Have you forgotten that's All Saint's Day?"

Frank said that he hadn't forgotten but that he really hoped that Father O'Donnell could manage All Saints this year without him. Frank was allowed three Sundays off a year, and he had only taken two, so he pressed his case until Father O'Donnell gave in.

"Why do you want this so badly?" Father O'Donnell quizzed him.

"To run the New York City Marathon," Frank answered. When he heard himself say the words, he knew for the first time, that he was really going to do it.

But for the next two months Frank would have to push himself physically, harder than he ever had in his life. The orthotics and the special exercises the sports therapist had given him made the pain in his knees bearable and he was determined to bear it, no matter what.

Frank began keeping the runner's journal on his computer again.

September 12th

Long-run day. Clear sky, about 60 degrees. Wore the heart monitor for the first time. Took me a while to figure the thing out but I finally got the watch programmed to pick up the heart rate from the band you wear around your chest. The band felt sort of awkward. I hope I get used to it quickly. And seeing my heart ticking away on the watch was strange too. Never worn my heart on the outside before.

Decided to do my long-run on the track so I could keep enough water handy and grab some every time I went around. That worked pretty well because I did it: ran 18 damn miles in 2 hours, 36 minutes. How do I feel? On top of the world!

October 5th

Easy 10 mile run today in cool, cloudy weather at an 8 minute pace. Kept my heart rate in the target zone and enjoyed the fact that I don't have to really push again until the 22 miler on Saturday.

Began to wonder what's pushing me. When I asked Eliot last spring if he wanted to train for the marathon he looked horrified, like I was some kind of masochist. Chris has gone away to graduate school, so now it's just me and my Nikes.

Maybe I'm running away from other things I should be doing, but I don't think so because so far I've managed to cover them all and in less than a month this race will be over. For better or worse.

No, I think I'm testing myself, testing my courage, and I think that will be good for other challenges that are bound to come along in my life, and help me help others face their challenges too. And it burns off sexual energy, plus I sleep better and I'm eating better. But I'm not sure where You are in all this, Lord.

There's nothing but silence coming from You. Why? Don't You want me to run this marathon, Coach? I can still give it up, at least I think I can, if You give me a big, obvious sign that it's not Your will for me.

October 21st

Wow, the human body is weird. I felt worse running 12 miles today in perfect conditions than I did doing 22 in the rain last week.

Maybe it's pay-back time for my knees. Stop doing this to us, they're saying with each step. Well, I will stop pretty soon, but not yet. And I'm still in charge.

It's made me think a lot about pain though. As far as I can figure out there are two kinds: the good kind of pain like working out your muscles, and the pain that kills you. But sometimes the lines between them are fuzzy.

Like Your pain, Lord, on the Cross. One of our parishioners asked me once if You were a "hurting" God and the only answer that made sense to me is yes, and no. You did hurt on the Cross, and somehow we believe that the pain of that sacrifice is made present in the Eucharist. Of course it's been transcended too and You have risen, but in another sense it's perpetual pain.

So, yes, You're a God who suffers for us. But not a victim-God, not a powerless God, but rather a God who holds His power back out of love the way the father in the parable of the Prodigal Son did.

The father didn't want the son to leave but he gave him the freedom. Does the father know it's going to be a disaster? That's not clear in the parable but clearly he knows it's been a disaster when the son returns. Clearly it's not what the father wants, and yet that's really an act of love on the father's part, allowing him the space to leave.

So I think to say You're powerless is on to a little tiny piece of the truth but it's poorly put and misses the larger point which is: when we're doing something and You seem to have no part in it, what's really happening is that You are leaving us free to choose.

That freedom You give us is love in its purest form because You leave us alone to make mistakes, and You leave us alone in a very dangerous messed up world. Which must be terrifying for You.

But You never give us more than we can bear, because You're always with us, guiding us in the right direction, nudging us in the right direction. In any situation, no matter how badly we've screwed up, You'll show us the way out. It may not be an easy way, but then again the Cross wasn't an easy way, was it Lord?

The reality of the Cross . . . it's message is that the way out is going to involve something dying in us.

The way out is the way through. We can't run away from it, we've got to go through it, we've got to carry a piece of our cross out the other side. And it's going to hurt.

Like my knees. Like running the marathon.

Chapter Eight:

All Saints

SHORTLY AFTER 3 P.M. ON THE SATURDAY before
the race, Father Frank checked into the YMCA on
East 47th street, received his room key and went upstairs
to unpack his gear.

It was the first time he'd been back to New York
since ordination, and the city felt both familiar and
strange to him. The Y was only a few blocks from
his old apartment and the bars where he and his
friends used to hang out. The broadcast studio
where he'd worked was just on the other side of Fifth
Avenue.

Would he meet anyone he knew on the streets of
New York this time, he wondered. Did he want to?

Frank hadn't kept in touch with his old media friends, and most of his college buddies had also left the city to settle down somewhere else. Maybe New York was a phase you went through, like puberty, Frank thought as he laid out his running things and put his Mass kit on the dresser.

He hadn't told his family or his priest friends about the Marathon, so he wouldn't be seeing any familiar faces in the crowd tomorrow either. This seemed to be something he had to do by himself, for himself.

But he was anything but alone. All over the New York runners were pouring into the city, excited, nervous, and obvious in their lean intensity and look of general disorientation.

Frank was glad he knew the Big Apple and glad he knew a cheap Italian restaurant where he could eat an early dinner heavy with carbohydrates. He bought a couple of bananas for breakfast from the corner market on his way back to the Y and was in bed by 9:30.

He woke early, too early. He looked at his watch and saw that it was only a little after five. Go back to sleep, he told himself, the more rest you get the better. But he couldn't sleep because he was too pumped up and his stomach was in knots.

So, while New York City was still deep in darkness, Frank laid out his Mass kit and began the familiar and calming ceremony of the Eucharist in his room at the Y.

People constantly asked priests to pray for them and Frank usually did so right after he was asked, in case he forgot. But he'd always had a nagging feeling that these prayers were too hasty and perfunctory, which is why he'd decided to wrap all his intercessions since he became a priest into one big intercession while he ran the marathon.

He'd offer up a prayer for someone with every step he took for 26.2 miles. Frank didn't know how many steps that would add up to but he figured God could work out the shortfall, if there was one.

The information that Frank had received from the New York Road Runners Club, the group that organized the marathon every year, said that the best way to get to the the start of the race was by taking one of the special buses that left from in front of the New York public library on Fifth Avenue. So that's what Frank did at seven in the morning of All Saint's Day. The race didn't start until after 10:00 but he couldn't hold himself back.

He elbowed his way onto a crowded bus with his gym bag and ate his bananas and drank a Gatorade on the way to Staten Island where the race began. The runner sitting beside him was full of conversation but Frank was too tense to process much of what was going on around him.

The marathon was finally, actually, happening.

Fort Wadsworth on Staten Island was already mobbed when Frank arrived and for the first time Frank focused on the fact that there would be thousands of other runners out there on the course, each with his or her own marathon dream.

The New York City Marathon was the biggest race in the world and the only one that was televized from beginning to end. There were the T.V. helicopters hovering almost at eye-level.

Frank pinned on his number and stretched as well as he could in the tightly packed crowd. His goal was to finish the race in under four hours, a reasonable time given his training times. But this would be different, he knew. This marathon would be run not just in his legs, but in his head, and in his soul.

At the cannon blast, Frank guessed that the front of the crowd was moving forward but where he was nobody could budge, so there went a couple of minutes off his time already.

Relax, he thought, for God's sake relax. You haven't even begun to begin. It's ok . . . you have no choice.

And for a split second he did relax.

Then the runners around him began to surge forward and he was off. He automatically started to pray but was too excited to concentrate, so he told his legs to pray and joined in the talk around him.

He heard someone saying that he'd always wanted to run the New York City Marathon but because it was on a Sunday he had never been able to.

"You work on Sundays?" Frank called across to him.

"Yeah, I'm a minister," the other runner said.

Frank laughed and told him that he was a priest. Now he felt more connected, more part of the scene and he tried to talk to the man again, but lost him in the mob.

"Pray for me, Father," a man to his left said as he pulled ahead. "I'm going to need it when I hit the Wall."

"I will," Frank yelled after him.

They were almost across the Verranzano-Narrows Bridge now. Frank looked down and saw fireboats spraying colored water below them. The pounding of thousands of feet on the bridge was deafening.

On the other side of the bridge, in Brooklyn, Frank got his first glimpse of the millions of spectators who lined the marathon route. He could hear a band playing and ran with the beat of the music, until the beeper on his heart rate monitor went off.

He was going too fast. Slow down, he told himself firmly. Keep this up and you'll burn out early.

After the first couple of miles the cluster of runners around Frank thinned out and by mile nine, which went through the Bedford-Stuyvesant area, he had plenty of room to go at his own pace and respond to the spectators who were cheering the runners on, yelling and giving them hi-fives.

Some people were holding up a sign that read: WE DON'T KNOW WHO YOU ARE, BUT GOOD LUCK! One of the runners next to him had "My Name's Dave" printed on his t-shirt, so lots of others in the crowd shouted "Go Dave!" as they ran by. Frank wished he'd thought of something like that.

There were water stations every mile of the route but so far he'd stopped only twice to drink. He knew he'd need more water as the race wore on but for now he was okay. His knees hurt, but he was used to that pain.

Now the race route wound through the quiet neighborhood of Williamsburg and Frank could see that the on-lookers were mostly Hasidic Jews. They were less exuberant than their Bedford-Stuyvesant neighbors but seemed equally fascinated by the spectacle of 30,000 runners with a helicopter escort materializing on their quiet streets. Some of them stood and watched silently, but others called out words of encouragement.

The next landmark the runners passed was the Pulaski Bridge into the borough of Queens, and after that Frank could see the awesome Queensborough Bridge which would take them into Manhattan.

Then the route made a left turn, and a right turn and the bridge receded again. It looked so close but it was still more than a mile away.

Frank remembered reading somewhere that the Queensborough Bridge was so long its builders had to take into account the curvature of the earth. He also knew that the bridge had a long up-hill and was impatient to get to the other side before the pain in his knees got any worse.

Taking his wooden beads out of the small inside pocket of his shorts Frank began to pray the Rosary. *Hail Mary full of grace, blessed are thou among women and blessed is the fruit of thy womb, Jesus. Holy Mary, Mother of God, pray for us sinners, now and in the hour of our death.* His fingers moved to the next bead but the sweat on his hand made him fumble and the rosary slipped and dropped onto the road.

Frank had to stop abruptly to pick it up. His quick movement almost made the runner behind bump into him, which could have sent them both sprawling onto the pavement. The man cursed at Frank and managed to pull around him to his left, but when he did so he kicked the rosary up the road ahead of them both.

Suddenly, Frank's priorities changed. He spurted forward, disregarding the warning beep on his heart monitor that told him his heart-rate was too high. Frank reached out his left foot, scooped up the rosary, grabbed it with his left hand, and somehow recovered his pace without falling. He'd keep his rosary clutched tightly in his hand for the rest of the race.

Finally Frank reached the Queensborough Bridge which meant that he was past the half-way mark. He checked his time: 1 hour, 49 minutes. Good enough to stop for water and a couple of bites of a Power Bar. He began to run again, this time more slowly.

All around him runners were slowing down or walking and there was an eerie quiet on the bridge. No one talked, no one joked, and there were no spectators to cheer them on. The up-hill seemed to go on forever, but at least the surface of the walkway was padded so they didn't have to pound bare metal with their feet.

After the long ascent of the bridge from Queens there was an equally long decent into Manhattan and everyone's spirits lifted. Walkers started running again and frowns of concentration were replaced by expressions of joy as the marathoners encountered the biggest and noisiest crowd of spectators in the race. A roar of welcome, like a blast from a giant boom box, rose up to meet them as they came off the bridge at 59th Street.

This marathon is in the bag, Frank told himself as he swung right onto First Avenue.

Why was I so anxious about it?

Ahead of him stretched a gradual four mile up-hill, then the Willis Avenue Bridge across into the Bronx, and the Madison Avenue Bridge back into Manhattan at 138th Street. Frank had studied the route the night before over dinner so he could picture it in his mind's eye. If only his knees would hold up.

He hit the Wall just after mile 22.

The pain in his right knee was acute now and his left knee was almost as bad. But the pain didn't penetrate his mind until fatigue and dehydration broke down his defenses and then it invaded in full force. Pain swept from his knees to his head, to the pit of his stomach like flames through dry tinder. This is the pain that kills, he thought.

Hail Mary full of grace, blessed art thou and blessed . . . is the . . . fruit of thy womb . . . Jesus.

What are the Divine Mysteries for today? It's Sunday, yeah ... it's Sunday ... oh yeah, it's ... All Saint's Day. Where are you Saints? Where are you God?

He'd never felt so lonely in his life, a kind of crushing loneliness, disconnected to anyone or anything. Even the rosary clutched tightly in his left hand seemed alien.

He tried to pray again. *Hail Cindy full of grace, blessed is ... are thou among women, and ... blessed is the fruit of thy womb, Jesus.... Holy Cindy ... Mother... Holy Cindy!*

He heard what he was saying, bent over and vomited.

"Maybe you should quit," one of the spectators said, moving out of his way as he staggered to the side.

"No," he groaned. "I just need water."

Another runner handed him a bottle of Gatorade. He drank some but couldn't keep it down.

"Here's water," someone ran to him with a paper cup. "Drink it slowly."

By now Frank was sitting on the curb. He drank the water and just sat there with his head on his knees. He had no idea how long he'd been sitting when he finally pushed himself back onto his feet. A couple of spectators helped steady him and he started walking forward again, very, very slowly.

Now, a kind of pulsating mist seemed to surround him. I don't usually see this way, he thought. This must be the pain that kills.

The pain that kills ... the pain ... that kills ... killed ... Christ ... the pain of ... the Cross ... killed Christ ... but that pain turned ... him back to God.

Where are you God ????

Where are you ... saints? You're supposed to ... be here today. St. Theresa ... Little Flower ... pray ... for me. See, I'm putting ... one foot ... in ... front of the ... other . . the way I taught ... Jeff ... Offering them ... up to God ... who seems ... to have abandoned ... me. That's your Little Way ... Can you offer ... something to ... a God who takes ... off ... when you really ... need Him. Did you ever... do ... that St.... Theresa? Yes ... I remember ... now ... you did.

St. Augustine ... you were a ... terrible ... sinner. One of ... the worst... worse ... than me ... but you became a saint ... so ... pray for me ... Don't you know it's ... All Saint's ... Day?

St. Paul! ... oh yeah ... the great ... St. Paul.... You said ... it's better to marry ... than burn ... well I'm ... burning up.

Frank's heart monitor went off again and he looked down at it through the mist and saw that now his heart-rate was dropping, fast. He tried to speed up but it kept going down. He couldn't get enough blood to his heart. Was he going to pass out right there on the streets of New York, in front of everyone?

St. Paul! ... pray for me. St.... Paul ... pray for me.... What else did you say ... St. Paul?

You ... said fight ... the ... good ... fight ... fight ... the good ... fight ... and something ... about finishing ... the ... race. Easy for ... you to say ... you were the ... great St. Paul ... for Christ's sake.... Christ! ... Christ ... Christ.

I can do all ... things ... through Christ ... who strengthens me. I can do ... all things through Christ ... who strengthens me. I can do all things through ... Christ who strengthens me.

The pain was a little better now and his heart-rate seemed to have steadied. Frank was limping but he kept moving, and Christ gently brought him back to God with every wobbly step.

The New York City Marathon finishes at the southern end of Central Park near the Tavern On the Green, an elegant restaurant that no marathoner has the energy or stomach to eat in, at least not right away.

Even the elite runners strain to make it up the last little hill, just 300 yards from the end. But the cheering crowd, the banners, the time clocks and most of all the knowledge that they've done it, draw them across the blue line where it's okay to double over, or collapse completely in pain or ecstasy.

By the time Frank reached the blue finish line the crowd had thinned out a bit but the cheers were just as strong. People seemed to sense that the runners who were still staggering over the last hill were the real heroes of the day. They were the ones who almost didn't make it, or never thought they'd make it, or made it out of sheer grit, or, in Frank's case, prayer.

After he crossed the line, Frank picked up his medal, limped over to a fruit stand and with two oranges in one hand, and a big paper cup full of ice water in the other, kept walking in slow circles until he couldn't take another step. Then he sat down against a tree and gave way to despair.

When he found the strength to lift his head a little he realized he was looking at a familiar pair of black shoes, and then a black overcoat, and finally, when he sat up all the way, he saw that standing there before him was Father O'Donnell.

"What?" Frank stammered. "How'd you get here?"

"By plane, haven't got my own wings yet."

"Well, thanks for coming, but I blew it," said Frank, looking back at the ground. "Missed my time by more than an hour."

"What do you mean, 'blew it'?" Father O'Donnell reached down and fingered the medal hanging from a ribbon around Frank's neck.

"What's this?" he asked.

"A medal."

"For what?"

"Finishing..."

"Finishing!" Father O'Donnell's face lit up with delight. "My God, Frank! Most people don't even begin."

Chapter Nine:

Advent II

November 29th

FULL CIRCLE, LORD. IT'S ADVENT AGAIN. **Full circle but it's always different. Each Mass has the same ritual, the same words, but somehow it's new each time.**

Do we get better at it? Is that how Your Kingdom is built? No, I don't think so. I can't imagine that it's our improvement because we always mess up, like I did in the marathon. Missed my goal by an hour, 17 minutes, but I finished the race, by Your grace.

I'm not a utopian. I don't have the delusion for even one moment that I'm somehow going to make this a better world. All I can do is try to point people to a better world by bringing little pieces of Your world into this world.

And I can herald Your coming, which is what I tried to do in my homily today. Advent can be a hard time for people, even Your people, Lord. They're so busy before Christmas and into all this busyness Your baby is expected.

Who's crazy timing was this? How can we get our hearts ready for a baby with all the extra shopping and celebrating?

But since there's no other place for Him to go we have to take the time to clean up our hearts before Christmas, throw out everything in them that's hard, or ugly or dangerous.

And then, as I warned the people of St. Anne's, stay alert, listen carefully, because this Baby isn't born with a loud lusty cry . . . but in the stillness of a miracle.

About The Author

Frances Winfield Bremer is the co-author of two other books based on in-depth interviews: **Coping with His Success: A Survival Guide for Wives** (Harper & Row, New York, 1984) and **Walk a Mile in Her Shoes** (*Niet Zeuren* in Dutch, Teleboek, Amsterdam, 1988).

Mrs. Bremer has appeared on *Donahue,* the *Charlie Rose Show,* and numerous radio talk shows. She is a member of the Literary Society of Washington, a former member of MENSA International, and the founder of the Frances Bremer Prize for American Literature at the American Embassy in The Hague. She is listed in *Who's Who in the East.* She and her husband are recent converts to Catholicism.

Running To Paradise
By Frances Winfield Bremer

FOR ADDITIONAL COPIES CHECK YOUR LOCAL
BOOKSTORE OR VISIT OUR WEBSITE:
www.prospectpress.com/html/books.html
OR ORDER HERE

Please send me _____ copies of RUNNING TO PARADISE
at $10 each, plus $3 shipping and handling per book.
My check or money order for $_____ is enclosed.
Please charge my Mastercard_____ or VISA _____.

Name: _____

Organization: _____

Address: _____

City/State/Zip: _____

Phone: _____ E-mail _____

Card No.: _____ Exp. Date: _____

Signature: _____

Please make your check payable and return to:

PROSPECT PRESS
609 MAIN STREET, BOX 162
SISTERSVILLE, WV 26175
or
CALL YOUR CREDIT CARD ORDER TO
PROSPECT PRESS: 800-685-0848

FAX: 304-652-1148; e-mail: Prospub@aol.com

NOTE: SPECIAL DISCOUNTS FOR QUANTITY ORDERS
ARE AVAILABLE FOR SCHOOLS, CHURCHES AND
ORGANIZATIONS. FOR INFORMATION CONTACT
PROSPECT PRESS.